She Was My Best Friend

Jealous: By Le'vonne

She Was My Best Friend

This is a work of fiction. All characters, organizations, and events portrayed in this novel are either a product of the author's imagination or are used fictitiously. Any resemblance to actual persons, living or dead, is purely coincidental.

©2020 Brand Bullies INC/ Brand Bullies Publishing

All rights reserved. No part of this book may be reproduced or transmitted in any form without written permission from the author. With the exception to reviewers, magazine articles, newspapers, and radio hosts who have permission, which may quote brief passages for public display.

Sale of this book without a front cover may be unauthorized. If this book is coverless, it may have been reported to the publisher as "unsold or destroyed" and neither the author nor the publisher may have received payment for it.

Le'vonne

Chapter 1:

Brandi

"Where the fuck you think you're going?" Nard burst into the bathroom, causing the door to hit the wall with a thud.

Pulling the curtain to the side, I rolled my eyes at the sight of Nard. He had some nerve bursting in here like a goddamn fool and I told him just that.

"I'm going to ask you again; where the fuck do you think you're going?" he enunciated. "You got your hoe gear laid out and shit."

"Nard, please close the fucking door. There's a draft and I'd like to wash my ass in peace." Pulling the shower curtain back closed, I continued to lather my body and scrub a dub.

Faintly, I could hear Nard still talking shit. He'd left out but clearly he also left the door ajar.

Le'vonne

Peeking my head out, my assumption was correct. Rinsing the suds away, I turned off the showerhead and snatched the towel down that hung over the rod. Without drying off, I wrapped my body and stepped out of the tub, making my way down to my bedroom.

"Where the fuck is my dress?" I questioned Nard, who was now sitting on the bed texting away on his phone without a care in the world.

"I threw that shit away. You may as well put on some pjs and kick back. You're not going outside with your thot ass friends tonight."

"The lies you tell!" I went back to the closet in search of an alternate outfit. Nard was out of his rabbit ass mind if he thought I was going to oblige his request. I was a grown ass woman and my daddy been dead.

"So, you just a disobedient mutha fucka tonight?" Nard tucked his phone in his back pocket and attempted to snatch the clothes I carried from my hands.

She Was My Best Friend

With the grip of a bear, I snatched them back in defiance. "Bro, I don't know what the fuck you on, but you can get the fuck out of here!" I spat. "You only get on this dumb shit when you're on bullshit. You afraid I'm going to run into one of your bitches?"

History had shown me that anytime Nard behaves like this, his inner hoe has reared its ugly head and he's doing shit he has no business doing. We've been fucking around long enough and as much as it has been apparent, our *thing* is toxic. Loyalty and being comfortable has kept me here. Don't get it twisted, I've done my share of shit too, but the money Nard dishes out allows me to be a stay at home girlfriend with a closet full of clothes and all of the bills paid. For that, I can deal with his bullshit.

"You my only bitch, but I got a trick for your ass."

Waving Nard off, I told Alexa to play City Girls. *Act Up* came bumping through the speakers. It was the perfect song for the moment. Rapping the words aloud, I grabbed some body butter and slathered it over my skin. By the time I was dressed and ready to roll, Nard was already gone and so were my fucking keys! I swear he could be a petty bitch when he wanted to be. Rather than get mad and act a fool like he wanted me to, I chilled, called up my best bitch and asked her to pick me up, omitting that Nard took my damn keys.

Chapter 2:

Mika

A night out with my bestie was just what the doctor ordered. This week of work has been stressful as fuck. A few strong drinks, some bomb ass wings and conversation with my girls was all I wanted with a side of dick.

Pulling up in front of Brandi's house, I called to let her know that I was outside. Moments passed and I was surprised to see her coming from the back of the building rather than the front.

"Why you coming through the alley? You had to take the garbage out?"

"Hell naw bitch, I lost my damn keys apparently and felt more comfortable leaving the back door open than the front. The rear gate has a digital keypad on it and can't no random just get in. That makes me feel a bit more secure in my choice."

Not seeing the logic in it all, I just minded my business and went with it. Knowing Brandi and her man Nard, ain't no telling what the fuck happened to the keys. Setting the car into drive, we glided towards our destination.

"Where you thinking about going tonight? Mr. G's?" Brandi questioned.

"Hell naw! Last time we went south somebody shot up the club. I'm staying my ass west of two-ninety," I stated matter-of-factly. "We gonna meet Junie up at The Sipping Room."

"Your scary ass," Brandi laughed.

Pulling up to The Sipping Room, we could see through the huge picture window that Freaky Friday was in full effect. Parks were so scarce that I had to circle the block a couple of times before lucking up on someone pulling out up the street from the bar. Flipping down the visor, I scanned my face in the mirror and reapplied some gloss.

She Was My Best Friend

"Best Bitch, you look good," Mika complimented my attire when we exited the car.

"You too Best Bitch, with yo' thick ass." Playfully, I smacked Brandi on her store-bought cheeks.

She wore a pair of biking shorts with an off the shoulder cropped top. Her long thirty-something inch weave swayed side to side as she walked. I donned a simple racer back wife beater and distressed blue jean booty shorts. My short red hair was pin curled, accentuating my high cheekbones.

"Have your IDs out and purses open ladies," the bouncer announced as we reached the door. Doing as we were told; he scanned our bags with a flashlight and checked our IDs before passing them back and allowing us into the bar.

The bass of the music thumped through the speakers, adding to the turnt energy in the bar. The Sipping Room was the place to be on any night of the week. The food was bomb and the drinks were strong. Plus, it was a no bullshit zone. The owner Hendrix didn't play that shit, and everyone respected him. We hooked up a time or two in the past. For the most part, we were super cool.

Pulling my phone out of my cross-body bag, I texted Junie to find out if she had already made it. The bar wasn't super huge, but it was big and packed enough that I couldn't just look around and spot her if she was there. No sooner than I pressed send, did she respond back that she was in the corner by the bar. Motioning my head, I led Brandi over.

"Hey hoes," Junie stood up from her stool and gave us an open armed hug. Already it was evident that she had been tossing them back. Whenever Junie got liquor in her system, she would get a little touchy feely.

Junie wasn't necessarily the third Amiga. She was a chick that grew up around the way with me and Brandi. Although she was cool as hell, I had to take her in doses. Junie was either up or she was down and that had a lot to do with childhood trauma. As much as I loved her, that shit could be extremely overwhelming to deal with. Tonight was a good night and I was certain we were going to have a grand time.

"What you drinking beautiful?" a husky voice spoke into my ear and slid his hand to my waist, as if we were cool like that.

Stepping back, I turned around and took in the facially challenged individual. He was fresh to death but ugly as hell. He smelled good but there was no way I'd be able to sit and rap a taste with him. My eyes would be on everything but him. He was more Junie's speed and I planned on passing his ugly ass right on over to her.

"Out of respect for my man, I don't accept drinks from random dudes. My fine ass friend right here single." I pointed in Junie's direction.

"Damn, you just passing a nigga around like a blunt, huh?" Ugly studied me. "She fine though, so thanks for the recommendation." Saluting me, he slid in on the opposite side of Junie and macked her down.

"Bitch, that nigga got money. Why you passing him off? And to Junie! Bitch you could have sent him my way," Brandi spoke incredulously in my ear over the music.

"B, you got a whole man. Plus, mafuckas know you Nard's girl. You can get your ass whooped if you want to."

"Whatever, Mika." Brandi gave me her back with an attitude and leaned across the bar, waving the bartender down.

I swear to God she gets mad at the dumbest shit. Not feeling her at the moment, I took the opportunity to slip to the bathroom. Walking down the dimly lit hall, I bumped into Hendrix who was coming out of the storage area with bottles of liquor in his arms.

"Long time no see you," I spoke sultrily.

"I know. You ain't stopped by to fuck with a nigga or to patronize the establishment." Hendrix flashed a knowing smile.

She Was My Best Friend

"I be working man. If I'm not working I'm sleeping. You know how that go," I offered an excuse and I didn't quite know why.

"It's all good. Drink on me," Hendrix held up the bottles he carried and left me standing in the hall.

Returning from the bathroom, I walked up on security putting Nard and Brandi out. The closer they got to the door, the more he yoked her up by the collar, half dragging her out the bar with Junie behind them yelling and talking shit. I could only imagine what I missed, and I was glad I missed it. Tonight was going to be good no matter what.

The music stopped and Hendrix's voice boomed through the microphone at the DJ booth. "If any mafucka in here think they going to disrespect my place, pour a drink on they man or slap they bitch up in here, you got the game fucked up! This establishment ain't like that other shit y'all used to. Conduct yourself accordingly or don't come in my shit. All money ain't good money and I have no problem banning mafuckas from my shit. Enjoy ya night."

The microphone made that annoying ass screeching sound when he dropped it on the DJ booth. Never have I seen Hendrix behave in any manner outside of cool. This shit was new to me. Now here my ass was at the bar solo because my stupid ass friend and her man don't know how to act. One thing for sure, two things for certain, their bullshit had nothing to do with me and my night wasn't getting cut short on account of them. With a now empty stool at the bar, I slid my ass up on the stool and took Hendrix up on that drink order. It'll be lovely if he gave me a side of dick. We'll see how the night goes.

Chapter 3:

Brandi

Nard did the mutha fucking most last night! While me and Junie was drinking with our new-found friends, this nigga come up out the woodwork showing his natural ass. In the midst of all the chaos and bullshit, I know Mika had to see and hear what the fuck was taking place. The funky bitch ain't even called to check on me or nothing. Fuck kind of friend was that? It's cool though because now the bitch on time out.

Sitting in this house staring at these four walls was driving me nuts. It hasn't even been a full day, but this Nigga Nard just won't let up. He's not trying to go outside with his sorry ass friends or nothing. I need an opportunity to break free and at this point I don't foresee one in my immediate future.

Le'vonne

"Won't you cook or something? Laying around like you a goddamn centerfold," Nard spat. "Ain't no need to be laying around looking all sad and shit. Had you not been hard headed you wouldn't be stuck in this bitch now."

"Bernard you are not my fucking father. That nigga dead!"

"You always hollering that shit. I am the nigga that take care of your ass and pay these bills. Feel free to get up off your fine ass and get a job. Then you can do whatever the hell you want," he stated matter-of-factly.

He gets on my goddamn nerves! I had one job my whole life and that was a cashier at Burger King. I hated that fucking job and although it wasn't the *be all end all,* it showed me that I was not about that employee life. That's why I got with Nard's ass. I was destined to be the woman of a drug dealer or a hard-working nigga at best.

I met Nard my junior year in high school when I got kicked out for fighting too much. After enrolling in CCA, an alternative high school, I came across the freshest dude in all the school. He was a year older; he had a lil' money because he sold drugs and he was very giving of all he had. We had what one would consider puppy love. He was my first and I loved him with all my heart and soul. Somewhere along the way we began to disconnect. Loyalty kept him with me, I suppose. I stayed with him out of sheer need. He provided a carefree world for me at the cost of having absolutely no freedom. I suspected he was hiding something or someone from me. My Aquarian nature wouldn't allow me to be restricted though, so we stayed having problems.

"What you want to eat?" I'd had enough of listening to his bullshit and since he wasn't going to have a mouth full of pussy, I may as well feed him and my damn self.

"Don't matter, just hook a nigga up."

Scrounging through the fridge and pantry, I gathered up ingredients to make T-bone steak, scrambled cheese eggs and skillet potatoes. Dressed in nothing but a t-shirt and panties, I stood in front of the stove. Feeling Nard's presence behind me, I continued to cook without acknowledging him. As I stirred the potatoes, green bell pepper and onion mixture, he began to knead my behind sending waves of pleasure to my nether regions, causing my slit to moisten. As mad as I was, there was no way I could deny him now and he knew it.

Turning the fire off beneath the cast iron skillet, I stepped out of the panties that he was now sliding down my legs. Forcefully Nard spun me around and hoisted me up as he slid in effortlessly. Locking my ankles behind his back I grinded on his pole as he walked me into the living room and stood me up on the side of the couch. In a flash I was bent over the arm of the couch with Nard furiously pumping in and out of me. Roughly he wrapped the ponytail I wore around his hand, yanking my head back causing a muscle to strain in my neck.

Usually a bitch was down for rough sex, but he was taking this shit to a whole other level. Nard let out a loud grunt and yanked my head even harder. He'd just bust a bodacious nut whereas I didn't get mine. Collapsing onto my back he made it hard for me to breathe.

"That shit was good," Nard stood up and smacked me hard on my ass. "Gone finish cooking."

Over-blew, I lay there trying to process the fact that this nigga just left me high and fucking dry! Unfulfilled with nut running out of me I wanted to cry. First he embarrasses me in the bar and drags me out like a defiant child. Now he uses me like a nothing ass trick. The sound of the shower could be heard down the hall. One side of me wanted to burst into the bathroom and act a goddamn fool. The other side of me decided to leave well enough alone. One thing for damn sure; if he thought I was going to finish cooking he had me fucked up. Something had to change around this muthafucka quickly.

Chapter 4:

Mika

"That's what your ass get!" I shook my head at my resident Mary Ann. All day she'd been bothering the other residents in the group home in any way that she could. Her recent ploy to trip her roommate backfired; now she was on the floor screaming.

"Miiiiiikkkkkkkaaaaaaaa help me!"

"I shouldn't do shit, you always messing with people Mary Ann, now look at ya." With my feet firmly on the ground I bent my knees slightly, grabbing both of her hands to assist her off the floor. "Are you going to leave people alone now?"

"Are you going to write me up?" Mary Ann questioned knowing damn well I had to write an incident report on the strength of her falling.

She Was My Best Friend

"You know I have to do my job. Can you come in the bathroom with me so that I can check for bruising?"

"Not if you're going to write me up," she batted her lash-less eyes at me as if it would win me over.

"Well, I'll take that as a refusal," giving her my back I walked over to my desk and took a seat.

"Black bitch!" Mary Ann spat, sticking up her middle finger.

"I love you too now go find you some business."

Supervising a group home of five individuals with intellectual disabilities can sometimes be extremely overwhelming but I loved what I did. There was nothing more fulfilling than being able to enrich the life of someone that was counted out and threw away. For a lot of people living in this demographic, they were born at a time when society deemed them as invalid and their families threw them away like trash, especially the white ones. Shit didn't make no kind of sense.

Writing the incident report to cover my ass in the event that she began to bruise or tells someone about the fall, I looked at the clock and saw that there was two hours left in my shift. Having not spoken to Brandi since the night Nard drug her from the bar, I took my chances on calling her. The phone rang one time and went to voicemail. My best friend could be a petty bitch when she wanted to. Either she was embarrassed or in her feelings. Knowing her it was more the latter. I hadn't done shit to her so there was absolutely no need for her to be mad at me. But that was Brandi for you. Either she was super sweet or super petty. Being friends for as long as we've been a lot of shit she does get overlooked under the guise of that's just who she is. This shit was getting old, but I didn't fuck with bitches the way I fucked with her.

*

She Was My Best Friend

It wasn't too often that I got off work early enough to do anything right after, especially hit up the grocery store. Although I lived alone, there was a need to keep my place stocked up at all times. Never knew when I'd have company or want to entertain. With my grocery list in hand, I entered Pete's Market and set out to find all the items I needed. The grocer was bustling with shoppers and everyone seemed to be in a hurry to get their shit and get out. My cart got bumped one too many times as I walked through the aisles and it was starting to piss me off.

"The isle ain't but so big, slow the fuck down and watch where you're going," I spat at the husky white guy that cruised the aisle as if he was playing a game of bumper cars.

"If you scoot your goddamn cart over."

"Muthafucka my cart is all the way up to the fucking shelf. Now slow the fuck down like I said. You got the right bitch today!"

Husky was about to say something else when a guy I hadn't noticed before stepped up in my defense. "Aye my man, just go ahead and roll your ass to the next isle and leave the lady alone," he spoke in an even commanding tone.

Without another word, husky went on about his business and I prepared to do the same.

"Are you okay?" the guy that came to my defense questioned.

Taking the time to actually look him over, he was tall with mahogany skin, and bow-legged. "I'm fine. Thank you," offering a smile I grabbed two bottles of pasta sauce from the shelf and placed them into my cart.

Walking away I put a bit of switch in my hips in the event that he was watching. Although I'd just gotten off work, there was no uniform and I was fine in my everyday clothes. Paying for my groceries, I left the store and headed for my car.

"Excuse me," someone called out.

I paid it no mind and kept walking because they could have been talking to anyone. It wasn't until the voice called me *the lady from the aisle* that I turned around and gave him my attention. It was Mr. Fine.

"I'm sorry to bother you but I was wondering if I could take you out sometime. I mean if you're not taken?" nonchalantly he glanced over at my hand checking for a ring I suppose.

"So, you speak up on my behalf in the store and now I owe you a date? Is that the reason you said something to ole boy in there?" I questioned pushing my cart towards my car.

"Hell no. I could have easily minded my business if that's the case. As a black man it is my duty to protect the black woman at all costs no matter the circumstances. I'm Christian by the way," he held out his hand.

"Mika," I took his hand into mine and noticed his manicured nails. Niggas these days didn't care about their up keep, good to see he definitely wasn't like those guys esthetically. The way he spoke with conviction turned me the fuck on, I can't front.

Pondering his previous question I threw caution to the wind and agreed to go on a date.

With a smile, he assisted by putting my groceries in the trunk of my car before exchanging numbers and bidding me farewell. Today was turning out to be a better day than I expected.

Chapter 5:

Brandi

Finally free from the lockdown Nard had me on the first stop was to the beauty shop. My hair needed to be done in the worst way plus I needed to put my ears to the streets and see what was going on around the hood. The shop was packed per usual and after signing in for my appointment, the receptionist let me know that my beautician was running late so I decided to go across the street to the store to grab some snacks. This trip to the salon could easily last up to four hours.

It was a beautiful day in Chi city, and I took in all of the sunshine. In a flash we could easily experience all four seasons in one day. Standing at the crosswalk I waited for the right of way before crossing the busy street. A bitch was looking good dressed in a pair of Nike stretch pants with a t-shirt and shoes to match. My mind drifted to what I was going to get into later today.

"Aye shorty…" some guy called out busting a U-turn in the middle of the street.

I heard him calling but kept stepping as if I hadn't. One thing I never do was walk over to cars that I don't know, and if a man wanted my attention he had to approach me. Hanging out of a car window making catcalls was not the way. Ignoring dude completely, I walked into the store without acknowledging him. Walking around the store I picked up everything I could possibly need and placed it on the counter. After paying for my merchandise, dude was outside the store leaning on his car. From my brief observation he had to be at least six feet tall. His gear and automobile screamed *MONEY,* yet niggas have fooled bitches before by way of wearing hand-me-downs and driving their homeboys car. Although Nard was the only nigga I'd been in a relationship with, he wasn't the only nigga

I fucked with. I had a type and my type was a man with money that wasn't stingy.

"Why I had to do all this to get your attention?"

"Excuse me?"

"You heard me," Mr. Attention stood up and closed the space between us. As I suspected he was well over six feet tall. "You got me risking an accident by busting that U-turn, then you basically said fuck me when you just walked into the store like a nigga wasn't trying to holler at you."

"Hold on Playboy," I held my palm up to stop him from coming any closer. Sex trafficking was real, and I wasn't trying to be a sex slave for no one. "I'm going to need you to give me fifty feet or something." My face contorted in an uncomfortable manner.

"See you steady playing me. I'm not used to no shit like this."

"And I ain't used to somebody I don't know being so close on me. I don't know you like that and in case you haven't been watching the news, bitches been getting snatched up."

Homeboy let out a hearty laugh as if I said something funny. Shit was real out here in these streets. "You know what shorty, you right. How about this," he held his hand out, "I'm Stylz and I'd like to get to know you."

Rolling my eyes, I dropped the tough girl role and took his hand into mine, "Hi Stylz, I'm Brandi. It's nice to meet you."

"Brandi... hard with a sweet after taste just like the drink. Miss Brandi I'm going to leave you with my number and when you're ready I'd like for you to give me a call."

Locking Stylz number in my phone I made my way back across the street to the shop feeling his eyes watching me with every strut. It literally was forty-five minutes later before Tela waltzed her funky ass into the shop. By this time there were three other clients waiting for her as well.

She Was My Best Friend

"'Bout time you got here, I was feeling like my dollars weren't wanted," sarcasm dripped with every word as she summoned me over to her styling chair. Tela was great at what she did but her work ethic sucked ass. Guess she figured no client has stopped coming to her in all this time, that none of us would.

"Brandi don't be like that. You know I be in this bitch all night doing hair. I over slept."

Sure you did, I thought to myself rather than speak it aloud. Fact was a bitch was ready to get beautified and get the hell on.

"Considering you and everybody else not trying to sit up in the shop with me all damn day I brought in some wigs that I've been working on for my new line," Tela began to pull different styled wigs out of her rolling luggage. "If you like one of these, I can still treat your hair and we can get you styled in a wig and out the door in less time."

Tela's words were like music to my ears. I didn't have all day to be fucking around, even if there was nothing for me to do once we were finished. As I looked through the merchandise I had the feeling that someone was watching me. Scanning the room, my eyes landed on a female that looked at me with a scowl on her face. Matching her stare she couldn't take the heat and turned away.

"Aye Tela, do you know the chick over there with the camo hat on?"

"Who?" Tela looked around just as I had previously. "That's Porsche, she used to fuck with Meek from over in K-Town. Why what's up?"

"She looking at me like she got a problem or some shit."

"Girl, she scary as hell so I seriously doubt she all of a sudden 'bout it 'bout it. Besides you don't know her so it shouldn't be shit."

Tela pulled a short blonde blunt cut from her case and held it up for me to see just as my cell rang. Nard's name illuminated the screen. Nodding my head yes, I connected the call.

"What's up?"

She Was My Best Friend

"Shit, why you ain't tell me you was going to get your hair did?" Nard questioned.

"What you mean why I ain't tell you I was going to get my hair did? How the fuck you know where I'm at?" no sooner as the question escaped my lips, I looked up to find Porsche still staring at me like she had a goddamn problem. Being one of the sharpest knifes in the drawer I put two and two together. Snatching the cape from my neck I got up from the chair and approached Porsche.

"What's up? You fucking with Nard?"

"Just so happens I am," Porsche smirked causing my blood to boil over.

Faintly Nard's voice spoke inaudibly through the phone while people nearby scooted away knowing it was about to go down. Without warning, I smashed my iPhone into Porsche's face causing blood to splatter from her nose. Reigning down blows, she didn't get a chance to defend herself as I pounced on her like a lioness. In the midst of the melee I dropped my phone, shattering the screen as

Le'vonne

Tela and another stylist pulled me off Porsche. Now that someone was holding me back she wanted to talk shit and act bad. Rather than give any more energy to the situation, I left the shop and headed to my car. Nard had some mutha fucking explaining to do.

Chapter 6:

Mika

My phone rang with a call from Brandi. Wanting to be as petty as she is I almost didn't answer but something in my spirit told me to pick up anyway. "Bitch what the fuck you want because you been super petty with me?"

I wasn't expecting to hear sniffling, that immediately put me on alert. "Brandi, what's wrong? Where you at?" I rattled question after question off not giving her an opportunity to answer.

"This nigga done embarrassed me for the last time MiMi," Brandi sniffled and blew her nose. "I'm on my way to your house." The phone went dead.

Well damn, I thought to myself placing the phone back on the coffee table. Wasn't no telling what Nard extra stupid ass has done this time. The song and dance they do in the name of toxic love was one that I'd never understand. As a friend I'll always have her back, but it was time for her to let Nard the fuck go.

In no time at all Brandi was ringing my doorbell. Opening the door she walked in looking busted and disgusted. Her signature weave was nowhere in sight. There were no lashes, makeup, nothing, just plain old Brandi. She rocked a fitted cap and Adidas jogging suit. This shit was realer than I thought. No matter the circumstances my friend is always put together. With my eyes trained on her, I watched as she slumped down onto the couch and pulled a weed pen from her fanny pack, taking a toke.

"So, what the hell happen because I'm not used to seeing you like this."

Brandi went on to drop a bomb on me that I wasn't expecting. Not only had she fought a chick in the salon over Nard. That same chick is pregnant by him and he kicked her out the house! My mouth was literally on the floor. What could I say to my best friend to make her feel better? What could I do? The sad part was that nothing that anyone said or did would fix the situation.

"Damn B, I'm sorry he did you like that. What the fuck are you going to do?"

"Your guess is as good as mine. Right now I'm staying at my mom house. I was smart enough to stash some money for a rainy day but it ain't hardly enough to set me up a place to stay until I find a nigga with some money to save me."

"Come on now Brandi, if this ain't teach you shit, it should have taught your ass that you can't depend on no damn man. Long as you been with Nard look how he did you!" My best bitch was absolutely delusional. In this day and age wasn't no niggas really out here weighted up like that and if they were, they still wanted their women to be self-sustainable. That was something Brandi certainly was not.

"Mika, I have no job skills. The only thing I know how to do is look good and suck a mean dick. That kept me straight for all this time."

"That run is over though B," I threw my hands up in frustration. "Not for nothing, I got an opening at my job. I'll hire your ass no problem. Then you can stack up for an apartment at least."

"I'm not working with them crazy ass people. The stories you done told me, and the shit you done seen, I'll pass." Brandi rolled her eyes in disgust. "I'd fuck one of them people up."

"You not going to be able to stay at your mama house for too long. Her mouth reckless as hell and she not just going to let you lay around in her shit and not do nothing." Trying my hardest to persuade my grown ass friend to grow up was fruitless so I switched the topic.

"You're more than welcome to stay here if you want but I got a date I need to finish getting ready for."

She Was My Best Friend

Brandi finally took the time to acknowledge that I was dressed up. She was too caught up in her own shit to even notice. "Damn boo, my bad. You're looking all cute and shit. Who is the lame?"

"That's the kind of mindset that got you fucked up now. Understanding that you're going through something right now I won't even go there with you." Leaving Brandi sitting on the couch, I finished getting ready. She could be so fucking shallow it was ridiculous. Rather than give her what she was looking for I switched my focus to the fine ass man that was due to pick me up within the hour.

Brandi was laid out on my couch when Christian arrived for our date. Something told me her ass was playing possum, but I paid it no mind. With my clutch in hand, I took one last look at myself in the body length mirror in the hall before exiting the apartment.

"Hello beautiful," Christian greeted me at the door with a bouquet of Peonies and a hug. The scent of Savauge assaulted my nasal passages in a good way.

"Thank you," butterflies fluttered in my stomach giving me the feeling of being a sixteen-year-old high school girl again.

Taking me by the hand, Christian led me to his car and opened the door. Looking up at my apartment window I could have sworn the curtains swayed indicating that Brandi's funky ass really wasn't asleep and just peeked out to be nosey. Nestled cozily in the car I eye fucked Christian as he walked around to the driver side and got in. Shyness was threatening to take over and I quickly pushed it out of my psyche.

"So, what are our plans for the evening?"

Putting the car in drive, Christian checked the side mirror before pulling out of the parking space and replied to my question. "For starters were going to have dinner at Mastro's, then go on a nice romantic carriage ride through downtown."

She Was My Best Friend

A smile graced my face, happy with our plans for the evening. In the history of never had a man thought this far and planned a date for me. It was either dinner then back to one of our cribs, or movies then back to one of our cribs. Not once did Christian lead on to us having to end our night with sex. However, at the rate he was going he could definitely get it.

"Check you out," I playfully pushed his arm "You're definitely trying to leave a lasting impression on a girl I see."

"That's the plan," he smiled showing a perfect set of teeth that looked extra bright due to the hue of his mahogany skin.

Ever since we met at the grocery store, he's sent me a few good morning beautiful and random texts throughout the day, but this would be the first opportunity for us to really talk. I ain't gonna lie I was intrigued by Christian. He was like a tall glass of that good brown liquor and my throat was parched.

Le'vonne

Valeting, the car Christian lovingly guided me into the restaurant holding the door open like the perfect gentlemen. On the surface he looked like a strong, hard-working man but I was wise enough to know that there was depth to him. After waiting a few moments the hostess led to our table near a huge window that looked out onto Dearborn Street. A waiter seemingly appeared out of thin air, introduced himself and poured water into our glasses, simultaneously placing menus onto the table before disappearing again.

"You are so beautiful Ms. Mika," Christian gazed into my eyes, hypnotizing me. Hanging on to his every word, I had to glance around the restaurant to shake off the trance he was putting me under.

"Thank you," I finally replied. "So, we finally get the opportunity to meet again."

"Yes finally and I want to know everything there is to know about you if you're willing to let me that far in."

She Was My Best Friend

Before I could reply, the waiter had returned and asked if we would like to order. Never having had the opportunity to dine at Mastro's before I picked up the menu and began to scan through it. Christian already knew what he wanted and asked if he could order for me. Giving him the green light, I sat the menu back down on the table and hoped like hell that he didn't order no bullshit. He ordered Oysters on a half shell as an appetizer with a bottle of Clicquot, an entrée of Alaskan Halibut, garlic mashed potatoes and creamed spinach for me. For himself he ordered a porterhouse with béarnaise sauce, lobster mashed potatoes and roasted Brussel sprouts.

"How did I do?" he wanted to know after he placed the order.

"You did good minus the oysters," I could feel my face balling up at the thought of eating what looked like snot in a shell to me.

"Just try one. I promise you your entire mind is going to change about them. Plus they are an aphrodisiac."

"We'll see."

Frederick returned with the oysters and champagne. After opening the bottle and pouring our glasses, he made sure that we were okay with the taste before leaving us alone. The oysters sat atop shaved ice on a silver platter with lemon slices. It was going to take more than lemon slices and Tabasco sauce to make that shit appetizing.

Christian walked me through the oyster eating protocol as he prepared one for me. Nervously, I watched as he squeezed a bit of lemon juice and sprinkled a small amount of Tabasco onto the oyster.

"You ready?"

Taking a deep breath I parted my lips and slurped down the oyster just as he'd coached me to. The way he watched me with bedroom eyes made my slit moisten. Usually I was a person that stuck to my guns and stood on my word, but with Christian I truly felt comfortable enough to let my guard down and follow his lead. That was something I'd never been able to do with any other man.

Over dinner, we were able to get very acquainted with one another. I learned that he was the oldest of two and was raised in Miami until the age of thirteen. His mother had moved him and his sibling here to Chicago with her family after his father was killed in a work-related accident. Christian didn't have any kids and owned a realty business where he flipped properties.

Opening up I told Christian just enough for him not to feel as if I was holding back. Life taught me to never give too much too quick, especially when it came to men. As a grown ass woman I didn't want to categorize him to be an average nigga. Everything about him and everything that he was doing was too good to be true. Niggas like this don't just fall from the sky. A bitch has to tread lightly as to not get my feelings hurt.

"Will you like to see the dessert menu?" Frederick made his way back to our table just as Christian leaned in and stole a kiss.

"Do you want dessert?" Christian asked licking his lips in an LL Cool J type of way.

"Only if it's you." Damn I couldn't believe I said that out loud. I could feel my face turning red in embarrassment.

"I'll be getting the check then," Frederick smiled and gave us a knowing glance.

Excusing myself from the table I dashed into the bathroom to gather myself. Not sure if it was the oysters or if it is Christian but I was extremely wet and horny as hell. Thank God I had sense enough to carry feminine cloths in my purse. After freshening up I returned to the table and Christian was ready to go and his mood had drastically changed.

"What's wrong?"

"Family emergency."

"Oh no! Is everything okay?"

She Was My Best Friend

"I don't know yet." Lines of irritation creased his brow.

With no desire to pry any further considering he wasn't willingly giving up any additional information. Our date was officially over. I could only hope our next meeting was as good as this one. There would be no busting it open for a real nigga tonight. Only Pornhub, and my good trusty vibrating rabbit.

Chapter 7:

Brandi

"If you don't get your lazy ass up and find something to do, we're going to have a goddamn problem!" mama screamed in my ear like she lost her fucking mind.

"Oh my God! What is wrong with you?" Throwing a mini tantrum I kicked and screamed like a kid.

"What's wrong with me? What's wrong is that I have been at work for eight whole hours. I come home and my lazy ass daughter is lying around my house like a fucking loser. You ain't took shit out to cook, you ain't cleaned nothing! Shall I continue?"

"Bro, this house is pristine. What is there for me to clean?" I questioned getting out of the bed. My mother stood off to the side with the most disgusted look I'd ever seen her give. Certainly she wished I were more like my sister.

"Brandi Marie, you just don't get it. You are a twenty-four-year-old woman. You should have a fucking career if nothing else. I love you to death, but you're not going to be able to eat, sleep and shit in here if you can't do shit or contribute to any of these grown woman ass bills I got. Don't none of this shit run on air."

My mother could be so fucking dramatic it was ridiculous. She always wanted to make it seem as if I was a lazy fuck up. That was part of the reason I low key couldn't stand her or my sister Paris. My sister was a college graduate, off in Seattle living her best life as a marketing exec while I was here in Chicago tarnishing my family good name. We were made to be different. She followed her path and I followed mine. My mother should understand that. Hell, I could be a bitch on welfare with a house full of kids but I'm not.

Not wanting to spend my evening hearing my mother bitch, I jumped in the shower and contemplated my next move. Hating the fact that I broke my old phone and it eventually got turned off due to Nard's none payment I couldn't access any niggas whose numbers were stored in it. Needing to get back on the scene, it was a no-brainer that a night out was on the menu. A bitch needed to be saved quick, fast and in a hurry. I stayed in the shower long enough to have my mother calm the fuck down and move on to caring about something other than what I hadn't done.

Emerging from the bathroom I heard my mother talking loud on her phone. My only hope was to get dressed and to dip out unnoticed. Packing a bag, I filled it with comfy clothes as well as hot girl summer gear. My night could go one of two ways. Laid back night or find a man and freak 'em night. Dialing up Mika I found out what she was on tonight and surprisingly she wanted to go out for drinks as well. Agreeing to meet her at her place, I threw on a pair of yoga pants and a T-shirt. Surely something in my bag would suffice for tonight's excursion.

"What the hell you going through that you want to come out for a drink on a work night?" I questioned as we ate jerk chicken and drank mixed drinks, waiting for Mr. Brown's lounge to convert from a restaurant into a nightclub.

"Work stressing me out and I'm trying to get my mind off Christian," Mika answered staring blankly into space.

"Who the fuck is Christian?"

"The lame," Mika chuckled taking a sip of her drink.

"Bitch, I know you ain't let no lame put you in your fefes. The horror of it all." We fell out into a fit of laughter. I told her about fucking with lames. Them niggas wasn't no better than the hood ones. Wasn't no man worth shit but his dick and money. "What the fuck he do that got you needing a drink?"

"He ain't did shit," Mika stirred her drink. "Our date was awesome; he was definitely up to get some pussy, but he wound up having an emergency after dinner and I haven't really spoke to him since."

"Chile, I'm a need for you to get like me when it comes to these niggas. Mama had 'em, mutha fuck 'em. Ride that dick and hit them pockets. Keep your feelings out of it."

"Brandi, I love you and all, but you cannot give me no kind of relationship advice. Sorry not sorry."

I was fucking appalled at Mika's response to my advice. The fucking nerve of her! One thing about me, any nigga that came close to smelling my pussy or not paid like he weighed. Bitch better be glad she got a meal out of him. The bar staff began to move tables around indicating the mood was about to shift. There was a dude sitting at the end of the bar that I'd had my eye on for a good portion of the night and I knew once the music started, I was going to smoothly sink my claws into him. He was a full-blooded Jamaican for sure or some kind of black island nigga. He gave off big dick energy and I could tell that he was somebody. He was just the kind of man that I needed.

Watching *Mr. Big Dick Energy* from across the room I took notice on how every guy that crossed his path dapped him up, while women were all in his face. He didn't seem interested in any of the women but that didn't deter me. They weren't me. Waiting for the right moment, I excused myself to the bathroom. Standing in the mirror, I ran my fingers through my wig and fluffed the curls back into place. My titties were sitting up high and my ass was bodacious and pronounced in my jeans. Adding an extra coat of gloss I admired myself one last time in the mirror.

"Excuse me," Big Dick Energy spoke in a thick accent as he narrowly missed running into me as I walked out of the bathroom.

Inwardly I was elated as I took this as a sign from God. He was shining his light down upon me from the heavens up above. With my hand upon my chest I feigned surprise.

"Whoa playboy. You might want to slow it down a bit."

"Slow it down you say? What you g'wan do if I don't?"

"Might have to put the foo fops on you," pretending to give him a two-hitter quitter, I demonstrated exactly what I meant.

"Tough gal you g'wan beat little 'ol me?" he laughed.

"Nah, I'll let you slide this time but be careful." Attempting to walk away he gently grabbed my arm and pulled me back in. Wanting to act out the infamous Napoleon Dynamite *YES* move I refrained and allowed my insides to smile instead. My little tough girl act worked.

"Don't run away from me gal. What's your name?"

"Brandi. What's yours?"

"Nigel," he placed his hand on the small of my back. "Why don't you come have a drink with me."

She Was My Best Friend

Just like that I was in like Flynn. Rather than leave Mika high and dry, I let Nigel know that I was there with my friend. He requested that I go get her and bring her back to his table in the back. Following the directive, I went back and carried out the plan. Mika sat at the table looking like a lost little puppy. The sight of her disgusted me momentarily. Home girl needed to develop a thick skin and stop getting caught up in these niggas' rapture.

"Bitch there's some fine niggas that want us to come kick it with them in the back. The quickest way to get over a nigga is to get under one so let's go."

"I ain't getting under shit but I will entertain a nigga to keep an eye on your ass."

Slapping fives, I waited while Mika grabbed her drink before leading her towards the area in the back where Nigel was waiting. The closer we walked towards the back a slightly familiar face came into view; Stylz, the guy that tried to talk to me was sitting across the booth from Nigel. Not for nothing, I never spoke to him outside of the day he gave me his number. At this point seeing him again didn't even matter today. A bitch was going to pretend she didn't know him and that was that.

"Beautiful!" a mile-wide smile spread across Stylz face. "I missed you. What you doing here?"

Feeling like a deer caught in headlights, my heart began to race rapidly. I couldn't believe Stylz was acting like we were like that. Preparing to correct him like we didn't know one another, I realized that he was talking to Mika.

"How you miss me and I ain't heard from you?" Mika questioned folding her arms across her chest.

Smoothly Stylz slid out of the booth and wrapped her up in his arms. *What the fuck was going on here?*

"Best friend let me find out you keeping secrets." Sliding into the booth next to Nigel I watched how the two of them interacted.

She Was My Best Friend

Mika looked to me before turning her attention back to Stylz. The music was too loud for me to hear what she was saying to him. Feeling kind of salty that neither of them paid my ass any attention. So many questions were running through my mind. Like where did they meet? Does he remember trying to talk to me? This shit was like The Twilight Zone.

Switching gears, I brought myself back to the here and now when I felt Nigel rubbing my leg. He could care less about what was going on just across the booth from us. Flashing him a sly smile he inquired if I wanted something to drink. Replying that I did, he ushered me out of the booth and to the bar. Nigel continued to get extra friendly with his hands as we waited for the bartender to take our orders. From where we stood I couldn't clock what my best friend was doing, and I couldn't wait to get back over to the booth to find out.

"Wha chu drinking?" Nigel questioned in his heavy accent.

"Henny on the rocks please." Making a conscious effort to put my mind back in the game and off Mika and Stylz, I began to whine my body to an old Dawn Penn tune. There was a script to be stuck to.

"Wha chu know 'bout dutty whine?"

Without a need to verbalize what I knew about it, I showed him. The DJ switched it up and threw Lady Saw in the mix. Nigel's strong hands gripped my sides as I backed my ass into his crotch, grinding to the music. With my eyes closed I became lost in the beats. With Nigel's third leg hardening it confirmed my feelings of big dick energy. Feeling a light touch on my shoulder, my eyes opened revealing Mika and Stylz standing before us.

"B, I'm going to leave with Christian, will you be okay?" Mika questioned knowing damn well she was going to leave no matter how I felt.

Astonished to find that Stylz was the *lame* Christian, piqued the fuck out of my interest. How small was this world really? I let Mika know that I

She Was My Best Friend

was cool. No doubt in my mind that we'd holler later.

A bitch needed answers.

Chapter 8:

Mika

What were the odds of me bumping into Christian coincidentally at Mr. Brown's Lounge? Thank God for Brandi wanting to get her hoe on and for me wanting to get out of the house for a while. There was no telling when I would have seen or spoken to him again. No longer the shy girl in his presence I inquired about why he'd been missing in action since our date. It wasn't like he hit and dashed on me, which had me feeling like I was a bore to him. Like, the chemistry we had that night, was it all a figment of my imagination? Unbeknownst to me, Christian had a mentally ill brother that went ape shit and had to be committed. Being as family oriented as I was, I understood.

She Was My Best Friend

Wanting to start from where we left off on our date, Christian suggested we go somewhere quiet to talk and a girl was all *too* willing to oblige. Brandi was caught up in her prey that she probably didn't care that I was ditching her anyway. Not needing her approval but it was girl code that we communicated our comings and goings especially if we were out drinking. Under normal circumstances I wouldn't have left her alone with a guy neither of us knew about. He was with Christian so he couldn't have been too bad. I don't believe that he would fraternize with suspicious characters. I don't want to sound like a bad friend or that I didn't have her back but fuck Brandi, because I was certainly trying to fuck Christian NOW!

"I missed you," Christian pulled up to my bumper and hugged me from behind, gently placing kisses on my neck as we walked out into the night.

"You sure about that?" I questioned glancing over my shoulder.

Le'vonne

The look on his face was apologetic as he spun me around to face him. In that moment the crisp breeze tickled my skin causing my nipples to protrude through the tank I wore exposing the fact that my nips were pierced. Folding my arms over my chest Christian's sly smile told me that he'd already gotten a peek. Knowing that he was going to see them tonight any how I dropped my arms and followed him to his car.

"We're not going anywhere until you forgive me." We stood on the sidewalk near the car.

"Boy stop it! I wouldn't have left with you if I didn't forgive you. Now open this door, so we can go."

"Boy?" Christian scrunched his face. "Ain't nothing boy-like about me. I'm a full-grown man baby." Switching up his approach, he apologized for the lack of communication once again blaming his familial issues for the distance.

She Was My Best Friend

"Mika, I'm serious when I tell you that I want to start over from here. There's something different about you and I fuck with you the long way. Let me show you that I'm not like most niggas,"

"Oh, I believe you. Understand I thrive off action, believing what I see over what is said. Honesty and loyalty is all I ask."

Leaning in for a kiss, Christian wrapped me in his strong arms, and I reciprocated by wrapping my arms around his neck. He was definitely getting some ass tonight! Breaking the kiss, he asked if we were going to his house.

"I have to work in the morning, so we can go to my house."

"Your place is nice and cozy," Christian complimented taking his shoes off and placed them at the door before grabbing a seat on the plush sectional.

Glad he had manners and I didn't have to ask him to take off his shoes. Cleanliness was one of my best traits and everything in my world had to be pristine. Besides, no one was going to walk over my white fury rug with shoes on period.

"Now that you got me here all alone don't be trying to take advantage of me," Christian joked.

"There's no need for that, you want everything I'm going to give you."

Ready to get the show on the road I motioned a come hither with my finger and led him to my bedroom. Flicking on the light my king-sized canopy bed came into view. "Why do women need fifty-eleven pillows on the bed?"

"Personally, I like comfort. I don't know about nobody else."

Unbuttoning my shorts, I allowed them to fall down to the floor as I pulled the tank over-head revealing my braless tits. Unaware of where all this boldness came from we'd come too far to turn around now. It had been nearly a year since my love below had felt another human. A good dick down was well overdue. Following suit Christian came out of every piece of clothing including his socks. My pussy jumped at the sight of his curved dick.

"Let me massage you so I can learn your body." He traced his fingers along my panty line and gently pulled them off before instructing me to lie across the bed.

Lying on my belly I waited as Christian retrieved coconut oil from my dresser and applied it to my back. The feel of his hands on my skin almost made me cream from his touch alone. He took his time to rub, knead, and caress every inch of my body. I even let him fuck up my hair to massage my scalp. By the time Christian had finished my body was in such a relaxed state it was damn near euphoric.

"You got any condoms?" Christian whispered in my ear gently applying his body weight onto me.

"In the bedside table," I panted. Regardless if I was fucking regularly or not there was always a supply of condoms on deck. You just never knew.

Better to be prepared than sorry. There wasn't any time for babies or STD's in my world.

Rolling onto my back I scooted to the middle of the bed and began to touch myself. Moans of ecstasy escaped my lips causing Christian to look in my direction. My eyes damn near bucked out of my head as I took in how much length he gained going from semi soft to hard. My mouth watered at the thought of pleasing him orally. I had to taste him before he slipped inside. Stopping him from placing the condom on, I got out of the bed and kneeled before him using my tongue to tickle from the base to the tip. I licked him like a kid licking cake batter from a spoon. He smelled and taste so good.

With knees as strong as Meg Thee Stallion's I balanced myself on the tips of my toes and sensually bobbed up and down on his pole leaving a trail of saliva each time. Singing praises, he gave me the confidence to continue to put my all into the job. Feeling the pulsation of his tool, I gave one last lick and climbed back onto the bed on all fours. We weren't at a place where I would willingly drink his babies. There was no doubt that he knew my freak number was high.

Face deep, Christian licked from my clit to my booty hole, blowing in my butt ever so often. The way he licked and slurped you would have thought that he was feasting on his last meal. After so long I practically begged him to give me the dick. The wetness of my slit allowed him to slip inside effortlessly, filling me up. Slowly he slid in and out savoring the moment. Gripping the bed sheet I tooted my ass up a bit more as he increased the tempo clutching my hips jackhammering my middle.

There are no words in the English language to describe the feelings I felt all over my body. Flipping me onto my back, Christian went down and licked my honey pot once again, sending me to a world I'd never experienced before now. I swear to god I had an outer body experience. When he slid back in I screamed in ecstasy as my body convulsed. With the noise I made I wouldn't be surprised if the cops came knocking. Stroking my G spot I squirted for the first time. Tears fell from my eyes as the gush of liquid flowed. Simultaneously he came with me, staring in my eyes all the while. This nigga had the potential to make me fall in love, or at least give me a bad case of dick dizziness. At any rate, neither was the lesser of two evils.

Chapter 9:

Brandi

With all the dick Nigel had, his big ass didn't know what to do with it. I was so fucking disappointed in our tryst I didn't know what to do. I lay in his bed looking up at the ceiling while he squealed and breathe like a fucking pig. Disgusted was an understatement. I popped my pussy twelve ways from Sunday, sucked his dick, and ate his ass only to not bust a drip of nut juice. Rolling out of the bed I stalked my way to the bathroom to bring myself to a nut and wipe my pussy down. Before I could make myself cum, Nigel was on the other side of the door banging talking about hurry up so I can go home!

Go home? Nah, I couldn't have heard him right. This pussy was too tight and sweet for him to think he was going to just dismiss me like I wasn't shit. Literally I might not have been but figuratively a bitch was the shit.

"Damn, I can't stay the night? Aren't we building and getting to know each other?" I questioned snatching the door open revealing the fact that my fine ass was still ass hole naked.

"No spennin' de night ma'am." Nigel hunched his shoulder and brushed pass me into the bathroom.

Incredulously I stared at his back as he soaped up a rag and began to wash his man meat. "With the way I just worked you over, you mean to tell me I have to leave?" I just couldn't believe this nigga was dismissing me like a regular bitch.

"Yea! Get dressed for dem leave."

Without another word I went back into the bedroom and picked my clothes up off the floor. With an attitude I slipped my shoes back on and grabbed my purse. Spotting his pants I made sure he wasn't returning before I slipped my hand into his pocket and pulled out his wallet. Rather than steal some of his money I pulled out a credit card that still had that sticker on it about activation. Tucking it away to use later I tried to pull myself together. This shit wasn't working out like I hoped. That was a problem. Before I left his place, Nigel texted away on his phone causing a massive attitude in me. The nigga acted as though he was mute all of a sudden.

"When am I going to see you again?"

"I'll call you," Nigel didn't give me any eye contact. All of his attention was still in that goddamn phone.

With the little pride I had left, I left his house with my head held high, slamming his shit behind me. Hoping to have knocked a photo or two off the wall. In the safety of my car, I pulled the credit card out of my bra. It was an American Express that looked to have never been used. Kissing the plastic, I dropped it in my bag and peeled off.

Back at mom's house, I inserted my key into the door to let myself in. The beeping of the security alarm halted my step as I hurriedly dashed over and keyed in a series of numbers hoping it would deactivate the system before the alarm blared. First I tried my mom birthday… denied. Then my birthday… denied. By then the alarm was blaring and my mother was running out of her bedroom talking mad shit.

"Why in the fuck is my alarm going off at four in the goddamn morning?" Mama snatched her robe closed and looked down the stairs at me as if I was a piece of shit on her carpeted floor.

The now ringing phone diverted her attention as she rushed down the stairs, "Put in your sister birthday to disarm the goddamn alarm!" she screamed before answering the call. "Hello… yes this is Ms. Jones, my daughter forgot the code. No need to send the cops… um hmmm… yes I'm sure. Thanks."

With an attitude I keyed in Paris birthday causing the alarm to shut off. My mother continued to talk shit, but I paid her ass dust, running up the stairs in hopes of running away from all the bullshit that plagued me. This wasn't a life that I could get jiggy with. For the first time in a long time I prayed for a blessing from the lord.

Two whole weeks have passed, and I haven't heard a peep from Nigel. A time or two I stalked Mr. Brown's Lounge hoping to get a glimpse of him or his car and pretend that we coincidently bumped into one another but no such luck. The little bit of money that I had was getting shorter and shorter right along with my hope of finding a nigga with some money to save me. They say niggas in these streets weren't getting it like they used to, and I was starting to believe it. Tonight was one of those nights where I had nothing to do and nowhere to go. Mika was at work, so I was subjected to hang with Junie's crazy ass.

"Bitch where you been? I ain't heard from you since Nard drug your ass out the bar," Junie laughed taking a pull from the Newport that dangled from her lip.

Her bad ass kids running through the house like wild banshees. Somehow she didn't seem to notice or just didn't give a fuck. With all the noise and bullshit taking place in this apartment it was safe to say my visit wouldn't be that long.

"Girl, I been soul searching and shit. I had to leave that nigga alone," I lied. "He was doing too much stunting and fronting. Had to teach his ass a lesson. Nard ass is on timeout,"

"You sure about that?" Junie gave a knowing glance. "I heard he got a baby on the way by Porsche from K-Town."

"Oh, really?"

"Yeah bitch and you fought the girl at the shop."

With a look of bewilderment I told Junie that I wasn't fighting no bitches over Nard and not to believe everything she heard in the streets because hoes be jealous. She claimed that she believed me but just wanted me to know what was being said. At the end of the day we both knew I was lying she just needed to go with what the fuck I said. Excusing herself to go to the bathroom I watched as her sons slap boxed in the middle of the hallway. These lil' niggas couldn't have been no more than four or five. When her daughter walked pass, the youngest boy tripped her and made her cry.

Junie came out of the bathroom with her pants unbuttoned and halfway pulled up on her ass, cussing them kids the fuck out. What boggled my mind was none of the shit they were around here doing bothered her until the little girl started crying. Let me find out she one of them favoritism ass mamas.

"Pooty and Boo don't make me fuck you niggas up! What the fuck y'all do to my baby?"

"It was Pooty mama, he tripped me," the little girl pointed.

That was all Junie needed to fuck little Pooty up. The way she swung her arms back and forth landing licks on his back I just knew he was bruising. The little boy screamed bloody murder as she showed no mercy in the whooping he was receiving. Unable to take much more of watching the baby get beat I got into their business.

"Junie stop hitting him like that bitch 'fore I call DCFS on your ass."

"Bitch call them. That shit didn't faze his ass. Please do me the favor cause ain't shit wrong with him," Junie let him go and as he ran pass me there were no more tears only maniacal laughter.

Whoo chile the ghetto! He was definitely going to grow up to be a killer. Chicago certainly didn't need any more of them.

"See look at his lil' bad ass," Junie took her seat on the couch breathing hard and shaking her head. "Them fuckers just like their daddy. Crazy as hell!"

Not wanting to talk about Junie badass kids no more, I switched the conversation to Mika. Since she reunited with the lame who coincidentally wound up being Stylz, I ain't really spoke with her. Either she was at work or she didn't answer her phone. With

She Was My Best Friend

Stylz acting as if he didn't know me there was no doubt that Mika was unaware that he tried to talk to me before.

"You talked to Mika? She got her a lil' lame ass nigga now and her ass been acting funny."

"Nah, you know Mika take me in doses. I'll probably hear from her next month some time."

"That don't make you feel a way?" I wanted to know. "Ain't no bitch about to deal with me on a sporadic basis. Either you fuck with me or you don't. Plus don't switch up on me when you find a nigga."

"Let me find out you big mad," Junie fired up another cigarette. "That's always been the dynamic of our relationship. It's consistent so no I don't feel a way. I'm not a person that most people can deal with every day."

Rolling my eyes I continued, "Well as her best friend I feel a fucking way. You don't dump your lifelong true blue for a piece of dick that's just going to throw you away when he done playing with you."

"Who said he's going to do that though? Look B, she grown as hell. Let that lady live and do her. As her friend be there no matter how it play out."

Over Junie, her logic and her bad ass kids. I decided to exit stage left and go the fuck home. I'd rather be in the presence of my mother and her bullshit than to be here. Go fucking figure.

Chapter 10:

Mika

"Alright ladies wash your hands for dinner," I alerted the individuals of the group home as I began sitting their plates out on the dining room table.

Once the table was set and they were seated I retreated back to the living room. I was eight hours into my twelve-hour workday, and a bitch was exhausted. I've done a doctor's appointment, gone grocery shopping, picked up med cycle change from the office and picked up the ladies from the day program. I was ready to go home and soak in the tub. Not having a dedicated second shift staff was taking a toll on me. On one hand I've been able to clock overtime. On the other hand, working so much was tiring me the fuck out.

"Miiiiikaaaa! Mary Ann is bothering me… Stop it Mary Ann!"

Rolling my eyes deep into my head, I slid my feet back into my slides and prepared to extinguish their fire. I was not in the mood for their shit or to write up an incident report if they got to scrapin'.

"What the fuck is wrong with y'all? Mary Ann leave Betty the hell alone."

"Honey tell her to chew with her mouth closed," Mary Ann retorted.

"Why don't both of you stop talking and chew your food? Look y'all I'm tired and I don't have time for the bickering. Can you please stop?"

"Yes honey."

Leaving them to their meal I retreated back to the couch. Working with people with intellectual disabilities was by far a hard yet rewarding job. They gave me the flux ninety-nine percent of the time, but I wouldn't trade my people for the world. The rapport that I have with them is everything, I learned early on in my career that when you give in to the bullshit they will eat you alive. I curse a lot when talking to them, but that's how I talk to most people. It's not out of disrespect it's me treating them like adults that know better. And they definitely know better.

My phone buzzed on the desk that sat across the room. In my mind, I prayed that it was not my third shift staff calling off. I didn't have time to be doing a call list and with the hours I already put in, there was no way a bitch was staying longer than needed. With no urgency whatsoever I slowly walked over to the phone. My attitude shifted slightly when I saw Christian's name on the screen.

"Hello."

"Hey, what's wrong with you?"

"Nothing just tired as ever. What's up with you?"

"Shit. Trying to carry that load if you let me."

"You trying to come work for me?" I half joked.

Le'vonne

"If I had it my way, you would never have to work again unless you wanted to. How was your day anyway?"

Back in my spot, I kicked my slides off again and told Christian about my eventful day. In the midst of our conversation Mary Ann got back on her bullshit, cursing at her housemates and acting a damn fool.

"Hold on a second… Mary Ann come here right now because clearly you're done eating."

"Yes honey," Mary Ann tried to play sweet.

"Yes honey, nothing. Will you please leave everybody the hell alone? If you're done eating please go take your shower and relax." Like a mother scolding her child, I gave Mary Ann the *do not fuck with me* look. As she walked away she kept turning around to see if I was watching her, and I was.

"My bad, now what was we talking about?" I redirected my energy back to the conversation with Christian.

She Was My Best Friend

He told me how beautiful of a human I was for working with people who have disabilities. My job definitely wasn't for the faint of heart. Ever since I was a kid I'd always nurture people, especially people who were *different*. It was almost like second nature for me. That carried over into adulthood and I'd literally had to watch over friends and men that I dated. Of them all Brandi was the one I felt most indebted to protect. After talking a bit longer with Christian about nothing, I ended the conversation with a promise to call him on my ride home.

Having left work half an hour later than I should have due to yet another incident with Mary Ann, a bitch was beyond tired. The thought of the thirty-minute drive that it was about to take to reach my house was blowing the shit out of me. All I wanted to do was wash my ass and go to bed. No passing go. No collection of two hundred dollars. Focusing on the journey before me I didn't think to call Christian back like I said I would.

Le'vonne

Turning on my ratchet playlist, I needed to shake my ass and sell drugs in my mind if I wanted to stay awake and get home expeditiously. Opening up the sunroof to let some air into the car, I merged onto highway eighty-eight and sped above the speed limit of fifty-five. The music and air was not doing what I'd hope it would do in regard to keeping me awake. Remembering that I hadn't put any money on my I-Pass account I pulled up to the tollbooth and prepared to pay. Thank God there was always change in my cup holder just in case.

Passing the attendant the money she thanked me and let up the gate so that I could continue my journey. With the recent updates made to the highway I directed my car towards the two-ninety ramp. Just as I merged a car came rushing across the lanes, I supposed not realizing the changes in direction until it was too late. In haste I attempted to speed up to get out of the way, but the car wound up hitting the rear right tire of my car causing me to spin. Thankful that no other cars were coming, I gripped

She Was My Best Friend

the steering wheel and prepared myself for impact as my car spun towards the guardrail. With the airbags deployed I cried out to God and thanked him for sparing my life because shit could have been worse.

Chapter 11:

Brandi

"Why you acting like our years don't mean shit Nard? You just throw me away for some random ass bitch you got pregnant!" tears streamed down my face as we stood in my mother's living room.

When Nard called me asking if he could come over I thought he'd come to his senses and wanted to work everything out. Instead he packed the things I'd left at the apartment in a plastic bag and brought them to me. We were truly done. I had no choice but to believe it now.

"Come on now B, you know this shit with us been over I was just trying to figure out how to tell you."

"How about you fucking say it! You don't just one day kick me out after the bitch you're fucking try me in the streets like I'm some punk ass bitch! That's what you don't do!"

"Don't act like you ain't did shit! I know about the niggas you was fucking with. I just didn't care enough to say shit."

Incredulously, I looked Nard upside his head. He was so fucking typical it didn't make any sense. How dare he turn this around on me? Enraged and wanting him to hurt like I did, I picked up a nearby lamp and hurled it at him. Any and all things that were near me were thrown at his head. Somehow Nard was able to tackle me to the floor. Still kicking and clawing at him, his bitch ass bit down on my jaw in an attempt to calm me down.

"Urrrrgggggh! You bitch."

Nard attempted to get up and run but I was able to catch him with a kick to the crotch. Able to get up off the floor while he held his genitals I ran to my purse and pulled out my mace and sprayed his ass up. I wanted the bitch to go blind. Nard cursed as he rubbed his eyes with his shirt, forgetting about his throbbing balls. In the midst of it all, my mother returned and raised hell at the sight of her house.

"WHAT IN THE FUCK?" Mama screamed dropping her purse onto the floor. "The nerve of you to tear my house up! Neither of you nigglettes pay bills here nor is any of the shit you're tearing up yours!"

"I'm sorry Ms. Jones but I just came by to drop off the rest of Brandi's things then she attacked me."

"I don't give a fuck," mama spoke through clenched teeth, her yellow skin red with anger. "Are you going to pay me for the shit y'all tore up?"

"Hell naw! Your daughter started this shit!" Nard snatched his hat off the floor and pimped out the front door, slightly limping as he rubbed his eyes.

"Brandi, you have disrespected me and my house for the last time. You need to get your shit and get out. You can't stay here if this the kind of shit you do."

She Was My Best Friend

"But ma…he…"

"But ma my ass!" she cut me off, "Clean this shit up before you go."

I watched as my mother picked her purse up off the floor and fished a cigarette out. Hot tears stung my eyes as I watched her step over the broken glass huffing and puffing on a Newport and talking shit. Here I was a grown ass woman and she still had a way of making me feel small like a helpless child. Cleaning up the mess I retreated to what used to be my room and packed up some clothes and toiletries.

In the comfort of my car, I dialed up Mika, my only hope. The phone rang and rang until it rolled over to voicemail. Ending the call, I dialed her right back, this time she answered.

"Mika, I need to stay at your house for a few days. My mama just kicked me out."

"That's fine. I'm here."

"Bitch, I love you and I'm on my way."

"Cool."

When I arrived at Mika's house, I was shocked to find her there with Christian packing up a bag as if she was going somewhere.

"Hey… you leaving?" I questioned catching Mika off guard. When she turned to me I saw that she had scratches over her face and a brace on her wrist. "What happened to you?"

"I was in an accident last night on my way home from work."

"Oh my God. Are you alright? Do you need anything?"

"Nah, I'm good. I'll be staying with Christian for a few days. Feel free to make yourself at home while I'm gone," Mika announced nonchalantly.

Again, the nigga Stylz was acting as if he didn't know who I was. He didn't say a word. Not hi, hey hoe how ya doing? Nothing. Retreating to the spare bedroom I tossed my bag into the room and went back out into the living room.

"Look what we have here," I spoke to Stylz who was now sitting alone on the couch. "Finally got you by yourself so I can ask the appropriate questions."

"Appropriate questions?" Stylz asked with a raised eyebrow, "Who the hell you supposed to be that you need to question me?"

"I'm her best friend and I need to ensure that you on something with her." Taking a seat on the couch across from him I asked my first question. "Question number one, why you acting like you don't know me?"

The vibe in the room became uncomfortable as Stylz stared at me. The look on his face made me somewhat uncomfortable but I didn't let up. He needed to answer my question.

"So…"

"So what? I don't like how you think I owe you an answer or an explanation to anything."

"You funny as fuck," I laughed. "You don't remember trying to talk to me? I mean you bust a whole U in the middle of the street just to give me your phone number."

The look on Stylz face went from confusion to comical. "Oh okay. What's up?"

"What's up? What you mean what's up? What you on with my friend? Your vibe screams player."

"Girl! I know you not in here questioning nobody?" Mika walked into the living room interrupting us.

"You know how I do, I got to make sure you straight and ain't no funny business." I looked Stylz square in the eyes. He needed to feel me.

"Dig, I ain't on nothing funny with her. A man knows a real woman when he meets her and treats her as nothing less." Stylz picked up the duffle bag that sat at his feet. "Baby, you ready to go so I can take care of you?"

Mika nodded her head with a silly ass grin on her face. "Alright B, I'm out. There is more than enough food in the kitchen. I'll talk to you later."

She Was My Best Friend

I watched as Stylz ushered Mika out the door. For some reason I felt the words that Stylz spoke to me was a low-key diss. He could kiss my ass at this point, and he was crazy if he thought I wasn't going to tell Mika he tried to talk to me.

Chapter 12:

Mika

In the days following the accident Christian truly stepped up to the plate and showed me just how solid he is. From the moment he found out about the accident he practically hasn't left my side for too long. The only time we've been apart is when he's had to check on his latest flip and even then he isn't gone too long.

"Put some clothes on and come ride with me," Christian announced when he returned from checking on his property.

Without hesitation I did as he requested. With summer merging into fall, the temperatures were a bit more comfortable making it easy for me to decide on an outfit. Within thirty minutes, I was showered and dressed in a Puma jogging suit with the matching shoes. Tossing on a hat and putting a coat of gloss on my lips I was ready to roll.

"Even when you're dressed down you look good," Christian complemented. "Damn you're beautiful."

Feeling like a schoolgirl with a crush, I smiled and licked out my tongue in a ghetto girl kind of way. Christian grabbed a handful of my cheeks and squeezed gently. He was trying to start something that wouldn't allow us to leave the house. Sensing that he let go and gave me a tap on the ass. Being with him truly had me feeling a way, in a good way. Deep down I hoped that this thing with us would last, and even if it didn't I was fine with the experience.

No need to question where we were going, I went with the flow and rode shotgun. Vibing to the music there was no place I'd rather be than with him. Turning the music down Christian asked me about Brandi.

"How close are you and 'ole girl?"

"Who? Brandi?" I questioned knowing he couldn't have been talking about anyone else.

"Yeah, her."

"I mean we been friends since we were kids. She's like my sister. Why what's up?"

Turning off the radio Christian looked over at me before placing his focus back on the road, "I tried to talk to her before. It wasn't nothing deep, very superficial. I gave her my phone number, but I never heard from her."

"You saying all of this to say what?" I shifted in the seat to look at him. More than listen to his words I wanted to read his body language. All appeared normal, no deceit detected.

"I feel the need to be very transparent and honest in my dealings with you. I'd rather you hear it from me and understand that I would never keep anything from you. That's why I'm about to take you to meet my mama."

"Your mama! I ain't dressed to go meeting nobody mama. Why didn't you say anything?"

She Was My Best Friend

"Don't be over there acting like you scared either," Christian flashed a knowing grin. "She's going to love you just like I do."

LOVE! Oh God. Did he just say he loved me? Panic began to set in as the realization of this situation weighed down on me. I really liked Christian, but I can't necessarily say that I loved him. I mean this shit was different. My stomach kept a case of butterflies when he was around, but love? Whoo chile it was getting hot in the car. Letting down the window my mind flashed back to the thought of meeting his mother. First impressions were everything and I didn't want his mother to think that I was some usual run of the mill kind of chick. I was dressed for the gym not for personal interaction with new folk.

I felt sick to my stomach as Christian pulled his car up to a house on the fourteen hundred block of North Lotus Street. It wasn't like I could back out, so I took a deep breath and followed Christian's lead when he exited the car. Waiting curbside, he approached me and grabbed my hand and led me down what felt like the green mile. I was that girl that was okay with dating someone without having to interact with any of the family members. I didn't need that kind of negativity in my life.

Christian used a key to open the door and held it ajar for me to walk through. The first thing I noticed was that his mom had similar taste as me. We both had an all-white living room with pops of color. While my color of choice was yellow hers was orange. Out of habit I kicked my shoes off at the door without having to be asked. Thank God my socks were clean. A nearby diffuser filled the air with bursts of a citrusy scent that was invigorating. Instantly I was at ease.

"Come on, let me introduce you to my mother," he kicked off his shoes and led me through the dining room, into the kitchen.

The smell of a home cooked meal comforted me even more and made me realize that I was hungry. A tall dark woman stood before the stove sprinkling spices into a pot as she swayed to the beat of Waiting In Vain. Scared as I was prior to arriving, I was liking this lady already without even having said a word to her. Bob Marley was one of my favorite artists and the song she was listening to was my all-time favorite by him.

"Ma, I want you to meet someone."

Startled she turned around and our eyes met. She was stunning. With high cheekbones and ebony skin like Grace Jones, she had this bohemian vibe about herself. She didn't look old enough to be Christian's mom at all.

"Son, you startled me," she wiped her hands on a towel before gently palming the side of his face and placed a loving peck on his cheek. "Who is this?" she looked me over as a smile spread onto her face.

"Ma, I'd like you to meet my girlfriend Mika."

Girlfriend? Lord have mercy. Me and this man haven't discussed being in a relationship. We were building to my knowledge. I didn't know how to feel. I was happy yet terrified. I didn't want the trajectory of this thing we had to change.

With a smile on my face and hand extended I spoke, "Hi, how are you?"

Momentarily she looked at the two of us and the smile on her face continued to get wider and wider. "My boy has never brought anyone home. You must be special. Welcome to the family. I'm Lovey but you can call me Ma."

Rather than shake my hand she lovingly pulled me into an embrace, and I couldn't help to hug her back. Instructing Christian to watch the food while we chat. She practically dragged me back towards the living room. In the time I spent with Miss Lovey chatting I found out that she'd always wanted a daughter but was blessed with two hard-headed sons instead. She also owned a realty company. Putting two and two together she was the one that put her son on to flipping property. From the look of her house and his I could tell that they made decent money in the realty game. When it was time for me to tell her about what I did for a living and how I met her son, she kept telling me how pretty I was, and what a great human being I'd been raised to be because of my profession.

About an hour into our conversation Nigel walked through the door followed by some plastic looking heffa with rainbow hair. Needless to say things didn't go anywhere between he and Brandi. Now that I think about it she never told me how shit ended up between the two of them that night. Guess she felt like she didn't have to say nothing, or some shit happened that she was embarrassed about. Either way, I made a mental note to ask her about it later.

"How come you bring company to my home without asking?" Lovey spoke in a commanding tone. Quite the contrast from the voice she used with me, and her son.

"C'mon now. G'wan with all of that," Nigel spoke in broken English.

"I tell you all the time when you bring these random people to my home. I protect my energy and the energy of my home always. Everyone is not welcome here," Lovey stood up from the couch.

Christian came rushing out of the kitchen diffusing whatever was about to pop off. He'd been quiet the whole time I sat and conversed with his mother, letting me know he was being nosey. I couldn't blame him though. I would have done the same shit.

"Unc, what's going on?" Christian's eyes scanned everyone in the room, lingering in my direction a bit longer. His eyes questioned if I was okay. I nodded yes in acknowledgement.

"Nothing nephew. My big sister tripping. I can't bring my lady friend by?"

"No, you can't! I told you about bringing random women to my home. This is family time. She got to go!" Lovey pointed towards the front door.

The girl looked as though she was about to act hard and say something slick, but Nigel quickly placed his hand on her shoulder and directed her back to the car. She protested but whatever he said in her ear got her to calm down and leave the house. Rather than give her the car keys, Nigel hit the remote to unlock the door for her. Couldn't have been me!

"So, let me guess, the simple woman going to wait in a hot car until we finish eating?"

"You no let her join. Where else she go?"

Lovey shook her head, "Son, go get your brother from the basement so we can eat. Mika help me set the table please."

Following the directives given I assisted Lovey with setting the table. She apologized for her brother's behavior, citing he has a habit of bringing random people over, knowing she didn't like it. I was a random person but who was I to tell her who could enter the home she paid for? Nigel made me uneasy with the way he looked at me as we set the food out. Lovey cursed him out in a dialect I was unfamiliar with. The only part I could make out was, needing to wash his hands.

A tall dark man that looked a lot like Christian emerged from the back of the house and took a seat across from me, avoiding eye contact with everyone while Christian sat to my right.

Lovey introduced me to her son Travis as Christian's girlfriend and instructed Christian to lead us in prayer. Astonished I listened to him project himself with the vigor of a pastor. Something about the authority in his voice set my soul on fire. I knew there were many layers to him, but this was a welcomed additive. I wasn't by far a religious person but with the way he spoke it was evident that he was a man full of confidence, and authority.

Before the prayer was over Nigel was stuffing his face like a wild hog, smacking and carrying on. The sight was extremely disgusting. With the noises he made, Christian stopped praying and cut an evil eye at his uncle. The night I met him I would have never guessed they were related. Not even now. They were like night and day.

"You ever had Curry goat before?" Christian questioned scooping what I thought was chicken onto his plate.

She Was My Best Friend

"Nooooooo," my eyes widened as I shook my head. I knew they were Jamaican but hell I wasn't expecting no damn goat. Where does one find goat meat in America? No store I shop in sells it.

"You going to try some for me?"

"What's the matter?" Lovey questioned, "You don't like it?"

"She's never tried it before," Christian spoke up.

Feeling like I'd been put on the spot to try it I rolled my eyes at Christian and prepared to eat a very small piece to appease him and his mama. I prayed to God that I survive this dinner as Christian cut a small piece and held the fork up to my lips. The smell of the meat was very inviting, but I'd been fooled by scents before. Like a G, I held my breath and closed my mouth down on the fork. The spices that coated the meat were pleasing to my palate. Breathing normally again I began to chew. I have to admit it was a tender and damn good piece of goat.

The smile that graced my face let everyone know that all was well and of course Lovey gloated about what a wonderful cook she was. I didn't necessarily doubt it either. Being from two completely different cultures, we didn't eat the same foods. Outside of jerk chicken, oxtail stew, meat patties and cocoa bread, I hadn't had the pleasure of feasting on any other Jamaican delicacies. Certainly I'll be experiencing more of the cuisine as long as I fucked with Christian.

When dinner was over I helped Lovey put the dishes away before we bid farewell. Nigel's lady friend sat in his car looking stupid as hell and I could only shake my head. I wished a nigga would leave me in his car for hours while he kicked the shit with his family. Oh well… their shit show, not mine.

"I think my mama likes you," Christian smiled leaning his head back onto the headrest before looking my way.

"I like her too," I admitted returning the smile before leaning in to kiss his lips.

She Was My Best Friend

Everything was going so well and although I kept flipping from being overjoyed to terrified about the entire situation, I made a conscious decision to ride the wave and let the chips fall how they may. Shit, I ain't had consistent dick and a man in a good while. A sister was going to enjoy all of whatever this is between us.

Chapter 13:

Brandi

I've been at Mika's house damn near a week and I've only seen her once. That was the day I showed up needing a place to stay. The slight conversations we've had haven't been about shit and they've been super short. With the boredom I've been experiencing I needed her to bring her ass back home. Dialing her number I patiently waited for her to answer.

"Damn bitch, did you forget about me?" I queried when Mika answered the phone.

She gave me some dry ass response about not acting funny but rather taking the time to convalesce. That was a sack of bullshit if I ever heard it. She was busy being under Stylz, Christian or whatever in the hell name he uses. I don't understand why it was so hard for her to call that shit like it was. Going with it, I told her that her presence was missed, and it would be nice if she came home.

With boredom covering me, I wished I could partake in my favorite pass time– shopping. With my money being as funny as it was, I remembered the credit card I stole from Nigel. In need of a new wig and some clothes, I went on Tela's Instagram page and got the website for her hair boutique. After ordering two wigs I scheduled and paid for a hair appointment with her via style seat. Fashion Nova was next on the list, they had a sale going on, so a sister was able to cop a few fits.

Knowing I had to strike while the iron was hot in terms of maxing the card before shit started declining, Nordstrom's was the last online stop. From them I ordered three pairs of shoes. Feeling better about myself I sent Junie a text to let her know that there would be a few deliveries coming to her house for me. Knowing I was homeless she didn't question the reasoning and I was glad.

Le'vonne

*

"Damn this pussy good," Zino sang my praises, as I bounced up and down on his pole.

Zino was a nigga that I went out with a few times, but it didn't get serious for obvious reasons. I was with Nard at that time and he was going through some things with his girl. We lost contact for a while but just so happen he ran into Junie and she gave him my number. When he called talking about wanting to kick it, I invited him to come over and watch a movie with me. Now here we were on Mika's couch fucking.

"You like this pussy, huh?" using my muscles to grip him I spun around in reverse, leaning my body forward clutching his ankles while still popping my pussy.

The angle you got from fucking on the couch allowed you to get more creative than you ever could on a bed. I was fucking this nigga like my life depended on it, and essentially it did. A lot of the shit that my mama, Mika and even Nard said to me about needing to get a job was at the forefront of my mind every fucking day. Zino was my last try at a savior. If he didn't bite a bitch was going to have to work. Thinking about it made me work my middle even harder.

"I'm 'bout to cummmmmm," Zino held me down and pumped furiously.

The way he pumped in and out, he found that spot and was stroking me right into a climax. The feel of his pole pulsating inside of me indicated that he'd reached his point of no return also. It was a win-win for the both of us. Climbing off of him, I went into the kitchen to get us both a bottle of water before disappearing down the hall into the bathroom. As I stood in front of the sink scrubbing my pussy Zino walked in and asked for an extra towel. Instructing him on where he could find one, I rinsed the soap and walked back into the living room to put my shorts back on.

My phone vibrated on the table, picking it up I saw a text from Mika letting me know that she was on her way home. Looking around, nothing was out of order but there was a wet spot on her couch and Zino's shoes were on her rug. Not wanting to hear her mouth and risk being put out of yet another place I picked up Zino's things and tossed it into my temporary bedroom before soaping up a rag to clean the spot on her couch. Using a blow dryer I began to dry the spot I'd just cleaned of my sex juice.

"Girl let it air dry," Zino stated watching me before taking a sip of his water.

"I am, I just want to dry it enough that it won't take too long. I put your stuff in my bedroom. We can go in there because my roommate on her way home."

Content with the cleaning of the spot, I rearranged the throw pillows and again took a look around and was satisfied with what I saw. Turning off the TV I crept to the bedroom and found Zino laid across the foot of the bed searching for a movie on Netflix.

"Don't go putting on no bullshit," I fluffed two pillows and climbed onto the bed placing my back to the headboard.

"We 'bout to watch some shit with a whole lot of shooting and car chases," Zino laughed.

"My kind of movie."

"Best bitch I'm home!" Mika's voice boomed down the hallway.

With my bedroom door open, I could hear two sets of footsteps coming down the hall. *Christian must be with her,* I thought to myself with my eyes trained on the door. His tall frame came into view as he continued to walk pass the room like no one was in it while Mika stopped and stuck her head in.

"Zino where the fuck you come from?" Mika questioned.

Zino let out a hearty laugh, "I be around. Just hadn't crossed paths with y'all. I'm back down though."

"Oh okay." Mika shot me a knowing glance. "Brandi did you miss me?"

"Hell naw. You wasn't thinking about me while you was gone," I half joked.

Sticking out her tongue and flipping her middle finger Mika disappeared down the hall towards her bedroom. For some reason my mind drifted to wondering what they were doing on the other side of the wall. It was none of my business, and I'm usually not pressed about what my friends got going on and who they got it going on with. Maybe it was the fact that Stylz tried to talk to me. There was no way that he would have known that we were friends. The way that I felt was making me a bit uneasy. Was it even possible for me to feel *jealous*?

Chapter 14:

Mika

State Farm didn't waste any time totaling out my car. They funky ass did put me on a short time limit to purchase my next vehicle with the insurance check. Although I was a simple woman, I absolutely had no idea what kind of car I wanted. Every car that I'd ever had was a Chevrolet, yet I was uncertain if I wanted something different in my life. Whatever the case it had to be reliable. Closing the lid on my MacBook, I tossed it to the side of my bed and went off in search of food.

Sliding the curtain to the side, I raised the kitchen window and let some fresh air in. From what I could tell it was a beautiful day in Chi City. The sun shined brightly giving my plants the rays they needed to thrive. Undecided on what I wanted to eat I took my time to look through the fridge and pantry to figure it out. One thing for sure, coffee was on the menu. Filling the water tank of the Keurig, I placed a Blue Mountain pod in to start the brewing process.

"Good morning; welcome back home," Brandi greeted entering the kitchen taking a seat at the table.

"Good morning hoe. How you feeling?" I questioned without turning around.

"Magnificent. You about to make breakfast?"

"Yeah. What you got a taste for?"

"Beggars can't be choosy. Whatever you decide is good with me," Brandi responded.

Finally making up my mind that I wanted homemade French toast and sausage, I pulled out the items and sat them out on the counter. As I whisked the egg, cinnamon and milk mixture I could feel Brandi watching me.

"Bitch you going to sit and watch me or help?" Glancing over my shoulder I noticed Brandi roll her eyes and shift in her seat.

She Was My Best Friend

"You got it," she shifted in her seat yet again.

Something about her vibe told me that she had something on her mind. Always one to have something to say, I wondered what could have her tongue so tangled that she isn't saying anything. With my curiosity getting the better of me I posed a question of my own.

"Considering we've known each other FOREVER I know when something is up so bitch spill it."

Brandi sat in contemplation before she finally smacked her lips and spoke. "I don't know how to tell you this, but your boo tried to talk to me," she finally confessed.

"He told me," I admitted. "I just want to know why you found it so hard to say something?"

"It's not that it was hard to say anything. You been around here like a lil' girl with a crush and I didn't want to hurt your feelings."

"It wouldn't have hurt my feelings at all," I stopped whisking and gave Brandi my full attention.

"As my sister I feel like you should have said something. I'm not tripping though. From what he told me you never called him no way so…" my words hung in the air as I hunched my shoulders.

"So, that's it? You okay with knowing your man tried to talk to me?" Brandi sucked her teeth. "For the record I questioned him the other night about his intentions with you. Niggas ain't shit and I would hate for your boo to have a harem of hoes."

"I'm aware but Christian ain't just some regular ass nigga out here. He's not in that same category."

"Girl you better wake the fuck up. Ain't none of these niggas shit. When he stopped calling your ass after y'all little date you was around here sad and stressed the fuck out. Then you run into his ass and now he not like other niggas? Bitch whatever!"

The attitude in Brandi's voice was very unwarranted. But this wasn't shit new with her. Every fucking time the light wasn't shining on her and what she had going on it was a problem. It was typical behavior and it was tired as fuck. I was over it.

"Chile, you need a hug and I'll give you one when I get done cooking," I spoke to Brandi's back, as she walked out of the kitchen leaving me to question where I stood with Christian.

*

"What you want from me?" I questioned Christian as he drove down Western Avenue.

He was taking me to a dealership where one of his friends worked in hopes of getting me a brand-new car today. So far, I was unsuccessful finding a car for the amount I was willing to pay. To be honest, I wanted to walk away with some of the money from the insurance check.

"Say what now?"

"I want to know what you want from me," I repeated myself.

"Where the fuck is all of this coming from?" he cut his eye at me as he merged into the left lane.

"Let me guess… from your funky ass friend right? What you think I want her?"

"You did try to talk to her," the rationalization left my lips.

"I didn't try to talk to her. I tried to fuck her! That shit has nothing to do with my feelings for you. Y'all two different kinds of people."

Christian's words hit me like a ton of bricks. If he wanted to fuck her when he first met her, certainly he had to still feel the same way. I was a fool to believe that he wasn't thinking about her or wouldn't hit, if the opportunity presented itself.

"What's the difference? We both got a pussy!"

"The difference is you're a real fucking woman. You have goals and aspirations. You got shit going for yourself. A bitch like Brandi don't want shit out of life other than to look good on some nigga's arm, be in bullshit and have a nigga take care of her. Don't no real man want a bitch like that!"

She Was My Best Friend

"You talking good shit but how am I supposed to know that you won't try to fuck her behind my back or if you fucking other bitches, for that matter," my frustration was high.

"Tamika, I took you to meet my mother. I ain't never took a woman to her. No one has ever been worthy of that. If I still wanted to fuck Brandi I could but that ain't me. If I'm with you that's what it is. You should never have to question my intent." Christian's words stabbed me in the chest as his words reverberated throughout the car.

My head was starting to spin, and I regretted starting the conversation. Christian looked defeated as he reversed the car into a parking space across the street from the dealership. Hot tears stung my eyes, but I refused to let them fall. How in the fuck did we get here? It was all good just a week ago.

"Look at me," Christian commanded turning the car off. With his hand he tilted my face in his direction. "Don't let your jealous ass friend come between us." His words hung in the air.

What did he expect me to say? I'd already let her come between us by initiating this conversation.

"Fix your face before we go in here." He let my chin drop from his hand before getting out of the car.

"Welcome to Kingdom Chevrolet, what can I help you with today?" a salesman greeted from behind a desk as we entered the dealership.

"We're here for Keithan," Christian spoke to the salesman as I stood off to the side looking like a wounded animal.

"You two can have a seat right over there," the salesman pointed to another desk with two chairs before calling Keithan over the intercom.

Silently, we sat deep in our thoughts. The tension was so thick with us it could have been cut with a knife. Pulling my phone from my pocket I scrolled through social media in an attempt to take my mind off my current issues. A tall light skinned man that I presumed to be Keithan approached. His tailor-made suit hugged his body in the right way indicating that he had a nice muscular build underneath.

"Stylz, what's good?" the man greeted with a half hug handshake. "This must be your lady?"

"Yeah man, this is Tamika."

Keithan held his hand out for a shake and I obliged by giving him mine. "Nice to meet you."

"What can I do for you all today?" Keithan unbuttoned his suit jacket and took it off, sitting it on the back of his chair before taking a seat.

After letting him know that I had A1 credit and was looking to purchase my car today with no financing, Keithan instructed me to look around to see what catches my eye. As me and Christian walked the lot I silently prayed that he would break the silence and say something other than a simple rebuttal after I'd pose a question about a car. After looking at six different cars, I found a black on black twenty-nineteen Malibu with a sunroof and power starter with no miles for just under sixteen racks. After reporting back to Keithan I learned that they had a sale on their previous year inventory so that they could make room for the new models.

When it was all said and done he was able to get me the car for fourteen five. Leaving me with fifty-five hundred dollars from the check. That money would be placed in my savings account for some other shit. Once that paperwork was signed, and my brand-new whip shined up I thanked Keithan for his service.

"Alright shorty, I'll talk to you later," Christian walked me to my car.

"I don't want to be into it with you. I just wanted us to have a necessary conversation," I pleaded with my eyes for Christian to understand where I was coming from.

"We're not into it and you're entitled to feel how you feel." Christian kissed me on the forehead and left me to watch his back as he jogged across traffic toward his car.

He was pissed and I had fucked up.

She Was My Best Friend

Chapter 15:

Brandi

I guess a bitch really had to tuck her tail and get a damn job. This wasn't shit that I wanted to do but it was oh so necessary. Zino was still fucking with me but he made it perfectly clear that he wasn't fucking with a bitch that wasn't doing nothing with herself. Since I'd seemingly fell off like bad dope and wasn't in demand, he was my only hope and so was Mika.

Mika was back at work and still looking for someone to fill the position she had available. It wouldn't hurt to apply, plus I knew she'd hire me for several reasons. One, she wanted me out her house, and two, she truly wanted to help me. With the clock ticking on me wearing out my welcome it was high time I cashed in my help ticket.

She Was My Best Friend

With my phone in hand I dialed up Mika. It rang several times before rolling over to voicemail. Never one to leave messages, I hung up and dialed right back garnering the same result. "This bitch be killing me acting like she so busy," I spoke aloud to myself as I sent her a text message asking her to call me back.

Minutes turned into hours as I awaited the callback I never received. With sheer boredom taking over, at some point sleep befell me. When I woke up I had a text from Junie telling me that some of my packages came and asking if I wanted to go have a drink with her. Shooting her a reply that I was down for the cause, I told her that I'd be by her place no later than ten. Opening my bedroom door I was confronted with darkness, indicating that Mika still wasn't home or locked in her bedroom at best.

Walking across the hall to the bathroom, I flipped on the switch and sat down without bothering to close the door. Reliving my bladder, I browsed through Instagram in an effort to see who was doing what tonight. Bitches were getting their inches installed while niggas were tearing the malls up. The people were going to be stunting in the city tonight. From what I gathered there was an after party following the Future and Meek Mill concert at The Congress Plaza Hotel. Tickets were a grip to get in but who said we actually had to be in the building. This was Chicago! The party could easily take place on a busy street.

Cleaning myself up, I replied back to Junie once more letting her know that I would be to her place sooner than later. We needed to devise a plan on how this shit was going down because a bitch was damn near on E in the money department. I would have to be as conscious as possible of my spending habits. Turning on the shower, I allowed the water to reach my level of comfort before stripping down and stepping in. The growl of my stomach enlightened me to the fact that I hadn't eaten anything since earlier today.

She Was My Best Friend

With an urgency to fill my stomach, I washed my ass quicker than normal. It was one of those situations where my hunger had me feeling sick to my stomach.

With my body still slightly damp I secured my towel and went back into my bedroom. Dressing in a jogging suit, I chose two possible outfits and threw them inside of my hoe bag. Doing a once over of the room to make sure that nothing I may need is left behind I zipped up my bag and prepared to leave. I could easily hit up a drive thru on my way to Junie's.

*

"Bitch, I told you all the niggas was going to be out here!"

Traffic was bumper to bumper as I crept to a turn onto South Michigan Avenue. Cars of all kinds intertwined with the flow of late-night downtown dwellers. The police were directing traffic and trying to keep the peace as late night partiers and hoes like me and Junie mulled about.

Le'vonne

"Bitch, I'm trying to find somebody to whisk me and my kids away."

"Giiiiirl them bad ass kids you got; I'on know about all that. You better rethink your plans and just find a nigga to fuck on and pay them bills you got!" I told Junie the truth not caring about her feelings. The daddies couldn't even deal with those BeBe's Kids so there was no need to look for a random ass dude to deal with 'em. Thank God it was only me by my lonesome and no baggage, technically.

"Hoe fuck you!" Junie spat. Evidently she was upset about my comments. "My kids might be bad, but a bitch don't need saving. I work every day and do fine taking care of my badass kids without the state giving me anything. What you got? I'll wait!"

Did this bitch just read me my rights? I thought to myself. The sound of horns blaring brought me back to reality and I continued to move along. Pulling up to the curb, I parked the car and we walked back down towards the hotel. There was no need to pay for parking in a lot or at the meter, we weren't planning on going inside the building so there wouldn't have been an issue with getting a ticket or towed.

With the intent on crossing paths with a paid nigga I wore a pair of biking shorts that accentuated all the wagon I was dragging while my tits sat up perky like in a cut off top that showed off my waist bead adorned belly and a peek of my braless tits. My bone straight inches fell well below my waist, while my face had a simple beat to show off my natural beauty. Thank God, it was unseasonably warm on this October evening. Junie wasn't looking too shabby herself. She showed off her curves in lace and spandex short cat suit. Her usually curly hair was now shaved close with a part on the side. The dramatic lashes and cat eye smoky shadow gave her an air of mystery. We looked damn good if I would say so myself.

"Girl, look at this bitch booty!" I broke out into laughter. "Should I tell her them butt pads shifting?"

"Hell naw I'm sure she feel that shit," Junie joined in on the laughter.

Two guys ear hustling on our conversation joined in saying that they peeped and when one of them tried to tell her she dismissed him as if he was trying to holler. Now he was willing to bet that her lopsided ass would make it to social media as a meme. The energy of the guys was light and the fact that their jewelry was gleaming it was a no brainer that these were the ones. Junie peeped game and gave me the look. There was no reason to walk any further we were going to finesse our way in. It was a plus that they both were handsome.

"Y'all cool as fuck. What's y'all names?" the thicker stature guy questioned. After introducing ourselves we found out that their names were Blaze and Teco. They were from Detroit and had come up for the concert and after party.

She Was My Best Friend

"Y'all smoke?" Teco the taller, thinner one asked. He was light skinned with dreads, a pretty boy and just Junie's type.

I was feeling Blaze, her reminded me of the actor Murda Pain in terms of his raspy voice, body shape and Detroit swag. Hood niggas was the type I like and he fit the bill. Just like the hoe I could be, I wondered what that dick and mouth do… rather than act thot-like I continued to converse and smoke up their weed. As the crowd began to get rowdy CPD pulled up on the scene with their bullshit. It was time to shake the tip but none of us were ready to call it a night.

"Where can we get something to eat at around here?" Blaze questioned sexily licking his lips as he admired my perky DDs.

"What you trying to eat besides my friend?" Junie chimed in calling Blaze out.

With a sly grin I licked my lips and asked if they had a taste for breakfast, something quick, or some hood shit. Given the hour of day that it was the only thing we could get is breakfast or hood shit.

"This y'all city. I just want something good," Teco rubbed Junie's backside.

"How we going to do this? We splitting up or y'all following us?" I queried bouncing my ass for the fuck of it.

"We can split and meet up at the restaurant unless y'all on something else?" Blaze questioned.

How we were going to do it was a no brainer for me, and Junie by the way we talked silently with our eyes. Although we were all hungry me and my girl were trying to hit a come up and clearly these Detroit fellas were trying to get some ass. Fair exchange wasn't robbery. Tossing Junie the keys to my car she and Teco went their way while I followed Blaze to the valet booth. As we walked I could feel somebody watching me.

Looking around my eyes landed on Nard and some chick that wasn't his baby mama. While he eye fucked me I switched extra hard and swung my inches side to side. I won't front and say that I don't miss and still love Nard because I do. But I'd be a fool if I gave him a piece of attention considering the way he played me with no regard. Laying it on thick, I fawned all over Blaze, rubbing his arm and what not while we waited for his car.

My eyes lit up with dollar signs when the valet pulled up in a white Tesla truck. No sooner than Blaze helped me into the truck I could feel my phone vibrating in my designer fanny pack. Pulling it out Nard's numbers illuminated the screen. Declining his call, I powered my phone down and pulled the safety belt across my chest securing it. Looking out the window I flipped Nard the bird as Blaze merged into traffic.

Blaze's phone rang and immediately it connected to the Bluetooth. It was Teco letting him know that he and Junie were heading to the hotel rather than grabbing a bite to eat. It was their thing and they could shake it like they wanted to. I for one was going to get a meal before giving up the ass. My mother taught me a long time ago that there was no way a woman should get up with a wet ass and an empty stomach. I did that shit once with Nigel and would never do it again.

Ending the call Blaze asked what I wanted to do. Directing him to White Palace Grill for some grub I made it very clear that I still wanted food. Taking our order to go we hit the liquor store and headed back to the crib.

Chapter 16:

Mika

I was supposed to go back to work today but it wasn't looking good. It wasn't that I didn't want to deal with my people, but a bitch was lovesick. There was no way that I'd be able to focus with thoughts of Christian plaguing me. In dire need of my village I called my supervisor requesting at least one more day and took a detour to see my two favorite girls.

Ever since my grandmother has gotten sick, she's been living with my parents. Being an only child, I'd always had a close relationship with my mother and granny. Needing their guidance and words of wisdom, being in their presence was the best thing for me right now. Although Christian is still speaking to me, it feels really different. We don't spend as much time as we used to and more than anything our conversations are really flat.

Ringing the doorbell, I stood on the porch awaiting an answer.

"Who is it?" my mother's voice seemed to sing from the other side of the door.

"It's me ma."

When the door opened my mother came in to view. At forty-eight years of age my mama didn't look a day over thirty. Many times people confused us for sisters rather than mother and daughter. With open arms she greeted me, and I walked into her warm embrace and sighed. It was so needed.

"Hey my baby! What brings you by?"

"Can't a girl just miss her mama?"

"A girl could but we're talking about you, *Miss Always At Work*. Wait 'til mama see you. Lock the door."

Doing as instructed I locked the door and followed my mother to the sunroom where my granny sat watching reruns of In the Heat of The Night.

"Hey Gran G," I greeted with a hug and kiss on the cheek.

"Chile, you look like you lost your best friend?" granny took notice calling me out as I stood before her.

"I didn't lose my best friend, but I did possibly ruin a relationship with a great guy because of my best friend!"

"What the hell Brandi done did now?" Mama questioned. "Elaine was telling me she was just living with her because Bernard put her out."

"Girl! Y'all stay gossiping about somebody. I hope you don't be telling her my business."

"You don't got no business," Mama took a seat on the chaise nearest the picture window.

With a need to lighten my load, I sat at my grandmother's feet and placed my head in her lap, laying my burdens down. Omitting nothing but the sex part, I told my granny and mother everything that was going on in my world.

"Chile… that heffa there!" Granny began, "Don't tell me her miserable ass done coerced you to be miserable just like she is?" Granny used the remote that sat in her lap to mute the television. This conversation was either about to get deep or take a wrong turn.

"Dang granny, tell me how you really feel." I wanted to roll my eyes but didn't feel like getting slapped, so I kept my facial expression under control. "You never liked her no way."

"I don't dislike a soul," Granny quipped. "I call things how I see it and she's been jealous of you for some time now."

"I don't have so much that someone would be jealous of me."

"Daughter, it don't take too much for someone to want your life. You may think you're not doing so much or have a whole lot but to someone on the outside looking in, you have it all whether you believe it or not."

"How is her telling me that he tried to talk to her indicative of wanting my life or being jealous?"

"Stop being stubborn chile. You just don't want to see what is before your eyes. One thing about it, God will certainly reveal the things that we fail to see." Granny gently rubbed my head as if she was engraining the words she spoke into my psyche.

"Mika we understand that you and Brandi have been friends since you were kids and that's because of my relationship with her mother. If me and Elaine didn't know each other or were never friends do you honestly believe that you and Brandi would be associated?"

Pondering my mother's words I couldn't honestly say that if she were some random chick from school or work if we would be friends. Me, and Brandi have always been like oil and water. Wasn't the old adage true about opposites attracting? Although I felt like she was the yin to my yang, could it be possible that I've outgrown her? Was my loyalty holding me hostage in this friendship?

"With you two being seasoned and all, how am I supposed to know if he's not full of it? Why would I not think that he's not still checking her out behind my back?"

"Baby, you got a lot of growing up to do. You're a full-grown woman but this right here is childish," mama waved her hand at me.

Getting up from my seat on the floor, I sat in a nearby chair astonished that my mother called me childish. I was more mature than most my age and didn't consider my conversation with Christian to be that of an immature nature.

"How am I childish mama? How would you have handled your man if you found out that he tried to talk to Elaine or any of your friends before you crossed paths? I'm sure you'd feel a way also," I reasoned becoming irritated.

"I wouldn't feel no way about something that happened before me. You said out of your own mouth that they met he gave her his number then crickets. She never called him. If she was interested in him and she called, and they hooked up then that's something to deal with. Seems like you should be more worried about Brandi wanting him now that he's with you."

"Baby girl, as an adult you are going to make your own decisions but please take the words that me and your mother are speaking into consideration. These days you young girls think that sex is what keeps a man or makes them want you. If he's a real man it's more about your mindset, poise, and characteristics. With you being raised by intelligent, strong and resilient women you and Brandi are cut from a different cloth and he knows that. You should know that also."

Digesting the words of my elders we changed the subject and started to talk about other things. Spending the day with my family was definitely what the doctor ordered because I felt so much better than I had earlier. When I finally gathered my bearings to go home my stomach was full and I had a plate stacked with food. With an overwhelming urge to speak with Christian I swallowed my pride and dialed his number. With bated breath I awaited an answer.

"Hey baby what's up?" Christian answered on the first ring.

My heart smiled at the sound of his voice, especially to hear him call me baby. That schoolgirl feeling began to overtake me. "Does this mean we still cool?" I questioned hating that it was even posed.

"You will always be my baby until you don't want to be no more. Even then you'll still be," Christian's words hung in the air.

"I want to see you… is there somewhere we can meet?"

"You ate? We can grab a bite and talk."

"Actually I am not. I spent the day with my family and of course they overfed me. I have an extra plate if you want to come by my place."

She Was My Best Friend

"That's what's up and yes I want it. I'm like ten minutes from your spot. How far away are you?"

The smile that covered my face was so big that my jaws hurt. Letting him know that my ETA was the same I weaved in and out of traffic in an attempt to get to my man. Turning onto my block I slowed down in search of a parking spot. Finding one across the street from the house, I merged into the space. Once parked I shot Christian a text to inform him of my arrival. In no time he replied back that he was pulling up. Looking through my driver side mirror I spotted Christian's car creeping up the block. Checking my face in the visor mirror it met my approval. Being effortlessly beautiful was a gift from God.

Today would be the first time I've seen him since the day we got my car. That was almost two weeks ago, and my soul craved him badly. Before I could think to get out of my car, Christian was at the passenger side of my car telling me to pop the lock.

"You not coming upstairs?" quizzically I eyed Christian getting super comfy in the passenger seat.

"Is your *friend* there?" Christian emphasized the word friend as he looked through the bag of food.

"She might be! Does her being there prohibit you from coming inside?"

With a straight face he admitted that it did, citing he didn't want me to think that he was looking at her or putting himself in a compromising situation. *Ain't that a bitch?* I guess I set myself up for that one. The theme of the night was definitely childish because his reasoning certainly was. If my mother overheard this conversation I wonder if she'd think he was childish like she said I was or just deflecting.

"What you come over here for if you can't even come inside with me to eat and to talk?"

"We can do all of that right here," Christian broke a chicken wing and began to smack on it. "I don't want no smoke with you, and I don't want you thinking I want your friend. I want you but you bullshitting,"

"How am I bullshitting? I'm trying to see what this thing is we got about, and where it can go but you taking a real ass conversation I had with you and turning this into something else."

"The only way this is going to turn into something else is if you take it there. I said what I said in our last conversation about ole girl and I told you what it was. Did you want me to lie? I'll never lie to you and I'm not about to walk on eggshells around y'all because she got you feeling like I tried to make her my woman or something,"

The shit Christian was kicking made sense, yet I was afraid to admit it. Guess my mother was right. I was childish and I'd made this into something bigger than it needed to be. All because of Brandi's ass! With a heavy heart the realization that shit might not get better began to set in. Why do I have to choose between the man I would like to build with and my best friend? On one hand it's like my friend has been my A1 from day one and has never done anything so drastic that I would just stop fucking with her. Christian was new to my life and I wanted to hold on to him for as long as possible but what happens if he breaks bad on me? Then what? I'd lose both of them if I choose him over Brandi.

"What do I have to do? Beg? This just doesn't make sense to me Christian."

Placing the bag of food onto the dashboard Christian stared me down, "You're so fine when you're mad."

"Are you fucking serious? This is not fun and games."

"I been told you that I don't play games," Christian rebutted. "How about you just move in with me, that way we won't have this issue and I know for sure that I wouldn't have to walk on eggshells."

"What? No… I like having my own space," I could feel my face twisting up.

She Was My Best Friend

"Fix ya face. You acting like I just asked you for a threesome or some shit. Tamika I know what I want and either you fucking with me all the way or you're not. Let's not waste each other's time."

Outdone and at a loss for words I allowed myself to sit in the moment and digest what Christian just said. Me, and ultimatums didn't get along. I was not a fan of people telling me what to do but I wasn't trying to lose him. Tucking my tail, I plead with Christian for reciprocity. Dropping his ego he agreed to spend the night with me.

Chapter 17:

Brandi

Waking up dazed and confused was not the move. There was a nigga in the bed with me that was not Zino. The one thing I was aware of was that we were back at Mika's place in the spare bedroom. Being asshole naked was an indication that we definitely fucked. I just pray to God we had sense enough to use a condom.

Shaking the rotund body that lay beside me, "Aye… Aye… Sir you need to get up!" Damn shame I couldn't remember his name.

"Come on girl, can't a nigga wake up on his own?" Pulling the sheet over his body he proceeded to turn over giving me his back.

She Was My Best Friend

"Dude get the fuck up you gotta go!" I exclaimed pushing his back one last time for good measure.

"Goddamn girl!" dude kicked the cover off and got up from the bed. "You lucky your pussy good and I want some more otherwise I'd go there with your ass."

As he stood on the opposite side of the bed the lyrics to Captain Hook played in my head as I salivated in regard to the thick semi hard peen with the left hook swinging between his thighs. *The lord is my shepherd, he know what I want…*With a lump forming in my throat I watched his thick ass get dressed. He was fresh to death in a pair of Amiri jeans, plain white V-neck tee and high-top Dior's. The sunlight shining through the window bounced off the diamonds on his chain and watch. Digging into his pocket he peeled off some hundreds and tossed them on the bed. I really think I like him, whatever his name is.

"What's your name man?"

Thickums chuckled and shook his head, "Should I feel like a cheap hoe right now? Because that's how you making me feel."

"I don't want you to feel like that, but I don't remember much of last night," I admitted.

"Blaze. Me and my homeboy met you and your girl last night at the Meek and Future after party."

Bits and pieces of last night began to play in my head, "Alright Blaze, I'm Brandi in case you forgot. Did we exchange numbers already?"

"Yeah, I got your number Brandi and you got mine. Come lock the door and call me later."

Nodding my head, I threw on a robe and tied it tight. No sooner than I opened my bedroom door we ran smack dab into Stylz and Mika walking down the hall. The look they gave me made me uneasy as neither of us said anything.

"Babe meet me downstairs, let me holler at her," Mika announced stopping right outside my bedroom door, looking me up and down like she was crazy.

"You can let yourself out?"

Blaze nodded and pimped down the hall towards the door behind Stylz. The intensity in Mika's eyes had me feeling that she was vexed.

"Who the fuck is that nigga? Brandi don't be bringing no random ass nigga in my crib."

"Bitch are you serious?"

"Dead ass Brandi. You probably don't even know shit about this dude. He could be a crazy ass killer!"

"Giiiiiiirrrrrrrl!" Rolling my eyes deep into my head I smacked my lips. "Mother Theresa don't act like you're so innocent."

"You lucky I have to go to work otherwise I'd go there with your ass," Mika dismissed me by way of walking towards the door."

"FYI, I applied online for the job yesterday," I called out behind Mika just as the door closed.

Knowing that Mika wanted nothing more than to have her house back to herself I made sure to inform her. Low-key letting her know that I was just as ready to give her space. Zino wasn't acting as if he wanted to live together so something had to shake, even if I had to get a job for a few months. Retreating back to my bedroom, the money Blaze threw at a bitch was tossed on the rumpled sheets. Belly flopping onto the bed I picked up the crisp bills and counted aloud.

"One hundred, two hundred... one thousand!" The nigga gave me a stack. Don't get me wrong I been knew I didn't have forty-dollar twat. However that little interlude with Nigel had a bitch momentarily feeling like my pussy was trash, considering the way he played me. Ole' Blazey boy was alright with me and I was definitely placing him in the starting line-up.

*

She Was My Best Friend

"Brandi this is Mary Ann, Donna, Virginia, Patti and Lorraine," Mika introduced me to the ladies that resided in the group home I'll be working in.

The house was clean and smelled good. The women were even well groomed. I didn't know why I was so surprised. With Tamika being the supervisor, I shouldn't have expected anything less. The thing that tripped me out the most was the clients were nothing like I pegged them to be. The people with disabilities that I'm used to seeing in the mall or wherever almost always looked crazy as fuck, and unkempt.   Not Mika's ladies. You could tell that she took really good care of them. The fact they were independent was a plus for me— no hard work. After shadowing Mika all day and being trained on daily data collection we were now kicking back waiting for quitting time.

"You happy I'm employed now?"

"What?" Mika cut her eyes at me. "Are you happy that you're employed?"

"No, I'm not, but I'm smart enough to know that you want me out of your space, and I think I'm ready for my own to be honest."

"Right now is not the time or place for us to be having this conversation," Mika dismissed me by putting the book she was reading up high in her face.

"So, when is the right time because you don't come home and you barely answer when I call you," I retorted. "Even right now you trying to son me like you that deep into your ghetto read."

Closing the book and tossing it onto the desk, Mika blew out a long-exasperated sigh and crossed her arms over her chest. The look she gave me was one I was all too familiar with. It was the look you give to a bitch when they're wasting your time.

"What the fuck you want me to say B? I'm going through some shit, and as you know when I go through shit, I tend to go into hermit mode and be to myself."

"Thing is you ain't been to ya self. You been under the nigga Stylz… Christian or whatever other name he goes by. Let me find out if you feeling a way over a nigga that I don't want by the way."

Mika had me fucked up if she thought she was going to treat me like a non-factor ass bitch over a piece of dick! Bitches like her made me sick. Your actions shouldn't be based off how a nigga feel. Shit, he came on to me not the other way around.

My words hung in the air before Mika replied, "What you not going to do, is act like I'm some gullible ass bitch that move funny style over a dude. Be serious Brandi. Secondly the interaction the two of you had before me is beyond me. Ya'll met that one time, y'all ain't fuck and you say you don't want him so what's the problem? While you sitting here acting like I'm treating you different because of Christian, please note that you been acting a way with me since you found out we were dating. So, what's really good friend?"

"If I've been acting a way with you trust I was returning the energy."

"Whatever B," Mika shook her head. "Look, I'm not going back and forth with you, especially not at work. We ain't never done this and we not going to start."

The doorbell rang, indicating we had a visitor. With the time being a quarter to eleven, it was clearly the third shift staff. Over Mika and her shit, I made up my mind that she and I would just coexist until I reach my goal then it's fuck her… and her funky ass man.

Chapter 18:

Mika

No… no… no… no… I shook my head as tears pooled in my eyes. This cannot be happening, not right now. In exasperation I sat down on the toilet and picked the pregnancy test up and looked at it once more. Again, all signs pointed to me being knocked up. One part of me was overjoyed considering my PCOS diagnosis. The other side of me was terrified. The revelation of me, and Christian having a baby can either make or break our relationship.

Soft taps on the door alerted me that Christian was trying to gain entry as he shook the doorknob "Babe, let me in. I gotta pee."

Without a second thought of wiping away my tears and hiding the evidence I opened the door and allowed Christian entry. "What's wrong?" he gently tilted my head in his direction noticing the tears that stained my face.

"Are you in pain? You don't feel good?..." Christian rattled off possibilities that would lead me to crying. When I didn't speak he took a look around the bathroom. When his eyes fell upon the pregnancy test that sat on the vanity, he picked it up and began to smile.

"Babe, you having my baby?"

Still unable to speak I shook my head yes. I was in a state of shock trying to digest the news. Christian dropped down to his knees and began to rub and kiss all over my belly. Speaking aloud to the fetus that he was going to protect and care for us by any means necessary. His words were like music to my ears. Again, a kid could make or break a relationship. By the way he was behaving, the addition was certain to be a step in the right direction for us.

She Was My Best Friend

Finding my voice, I wiped away the tears. "I thought you had to pee."

"I do but the two of you are more important. Do you know how far along you are?"

Taking a seat on the edge of the tub while he peed I let him know that I would have to make a doctor's appointment to find out although I couldn't have been more than a month. Missing a period was normal in my world of PCOS so when I didn't bleed for two months straight it wasn't enough to alarm me. Truth of the matter is, I had no reason to believe I was pregnant. Sure I'd been moody, had tender breast, was overly exhausted and my sense of smell picked up tremendously. Even then the thought didn't cross my mind until Junie pointed some things out to me, mainly the heaviness of my breast. They'd seemingly grown in size and no matter how much I drank coffee or red bull's I was always overly lethargic. With all the kids Junie had, I knew she was on to something and decided to take a test. Low key I didn't think I could have kids. I know that sound stupid but a lot of women with the same disorder as me had a hard time conceiving and if they did it more often than not ended in miscarriage.

The realization that I might lose the child hit me like a ton of bricks. How can I get excited about something that may get snatched away from me? Just as quickly as I got excited I began to feel terrible. Christian was excited and ready to shout from the rooftops that he was going to be a dad. I didn't want to disappoint him, but things may not pan out the way he hoped. Not wanting to piss on his parade, I allowed him to have his moment and kept my mouth shut.

After cleaning his self-up, Christian whisked me off my feet and carried me back to the bedroom. Gently placing me on the bed, he climbed up between my legs and planted a trail of kisses from my thighs to my honey pot. The heat from his breath tickled my skin as his tongue flicked my love button. Gripping the sheets my body quaked as I came. With a glazed face, Christian came up for air and kissed my lips allowing me to taste my own nectar.

Wanting to please him, I told Christian to lie on his back. Instead of obliging my request, he told me that tonight was all about me. Guiding me to turn over, arching my back I tooted my ass in the air giving full access.

"Bae this pussy so good..." Christian slowly slid in and stroked my spot causing me to emit a deep moan. Hitting the bottom, the feel of his love between my thighs made me scream out in pleasure.

Crumpling the bed sheets within the clutches of my fists I screamed out as my body began to convulse. Sex with Christian was always so amazing. In the few short months that we've been dealing he's given me a new lease on life, and I loved it. I was evolving and growing more into my womanhood.

"You ready to come for me Bae?"

Nodding my head because my voice box was weak from the moaning and screaming I'd done; he gripped my shoulders as I threw my ass back at him.

Le'vonne

The sound of our skin slapping reverberated off the walls as Christian groaned spilling his seed deep within my womb. The contracting of my vaginal muscles gripped his tool as I gently wound my middle. Panting in my ear, Christian licked my lobe and laid his weight on my back before rolling over onto the bed.

"It's your turn to get the rag," I lay flat on my stomach prepared to go to la la land.

"Fuck them rags. Come cuddle with me," Christian commanded.

Although I didn't care to lay with sticky icky between my thighs I was too tired to get a rag. Compliantly I crawled over until I was lying with my head on his chest and fell asleep to the sound of his heartbeat.

*

We'd spent the better half of today at the doctor confirming my pregnancy. Just as I suspected, I was at least six weeks along. My doctor did a great job of helping to ease my anxiety in regard to

She Was My Best Friend

possibly miscarrying due to my Polycystic Ovarian Syndrome diagnosis. Christian was so excited about being a dad that he was telling anyone willing to listen that I was carrying his son. Who said it was a boy? If anything my little princess was going to have the both of us wrapped around her perfect little fingers. Feeling better about my situation I thought there was no better time than the present for my immediate family to meet the father of my child.

Dialing up my mother, I made sure that she was home. With today being Saturday she could have easily been out shopping or doing whatever it was she did these days. Good thing dad was home also so we can knock this surprise out in one wop. Nervousness caused my palms to sweat as I wondered the level of disappointment that my parents may exude. I was their only child and their expectation level of me has always been high.

"Are you going to be okay?" Christian questioned in regard to the change in my demeanor after ending the call with my mother.

"I hope so," I admitted. "I'm starting to feel sick to my stomach," crouching down in the passenger seat I began to moan and rub my belly.

"You better not throw up in my car," Christian half joked switching lanes.

Rather than replying to my ignorant ass baby daddy, I stuck my middle finger up and licked out my tongue. When we pulled up in front of my childhood home daddy was raking the freshly fallen autumn leaves. Taking a deep breath I squeezed Christian's hand tightly and instructed him to follow me. Side by side we walked the pathway that led up to the house.

"Hey, Daddy, I have someone I want you to meet."

Sliding his glasses down to the rim of his nose, daddy studied Christian over the rims of his specks. Not intimidated by the stare my father gave, I watched as Christian walked over and introduced himself with a firm handshake. He even offered to help, and daddy didn't dare decline. Knowing that he could hold his own I left them in the yard while I went off in search of my two favorite girls. Per usual I found them in the sunroom. They were repotting plants and gossiping.

"Y'all always talking about somebody. Mess around and get beat up!"

"Please! Don't nobody want no static with me and my daughter. Matter of fact, your ass better jump in too!" Grandma wiped her hands on her smock and gave me a hug.

After she released me she seemed to study my presence and it made me uncomfortable. It was as if she knew what was up. Spinning on the ball of my foot, I leaned over and kissed my mother on the cheek before taking a seat in a nearby chair. Although I wasn't showing yet, I wore an oversized hoodie that I kept pulling away from my belly as if it was telling my secret.

"I brought somebody over here to meet you cool kittens. He outside with daddy."

"Ma you hear this?" Mama stopped pouring dirt in the pot that sat between her legs. "I guess our conversation worked and this girl went and got her man."

"He better be fine or we going to talk about the ugly nigga when you leave," Grandma cackled, and I didn't find shit funny.

"Granny let's not get into it because when you see him that old Thunder cat might start purring down there. Just know he don't do cougars and jaguars only young tender thangs such as myself."

"I guess you told me! Janet hurry up with that plant so we can go see Magilla."

Bursting into a fit of laughter mama almost dropped the Maranta she'd just repotted. Playfully rolling my eyes I stood up from my seat when I heard the side door open. Knowing daddy and Christian were now in the house I was anxious to find out how well they were getting along or not. Going off in search of the men I could hear my grandmother talking mad shit as she and mom followed behind me.

She Was My Best Friend

"Has my dad been easy on you?" I questioned kissing Christian on the cheek and sat next to him on a stool at the kitchen island. There was no feel of tension in the air, so it was safe to say that things went well with the two of them.

"I go easy on no one when it comes to my baby girl," dad interjected. "Christian seems to have his head on his shoulders yet in fatherly fashion I have my eye on him," daddy winked and opened up the fridge pulling out his usual ginger ale.

"Mom… grandmother, this is my boyfriend Christian."

"Nice to meet you. We've heard so much about you," mom chimed in while granny smiled like a Cheshire cat.

"Likewise Mrs. Smith… grandmother Smith," Christian kissed both of their hands.

"Is your mother still with your daddy? I'm looking for a new man," grandma joked.

"Ma! Christian pay her no mind," mama apologized for our heat filled matriarch.

"My father is deceased and you too good for my uncle and brother," Christian replied easing the tension that could have easily crept in.

"Good looking," grandma laughed. "If you find a young tender thing that'll treat me right you send him over, okay? He has to be like you though."

Agreeing, Christian laughed and told me how much he liked my grandmother.

So far so good I thought to myself as my family asked Christian questions about his upbringing and current status. I could tell that they were impressed with the answers he was giving them. I know my dad certainly was. He always wanted nothing more than for me to have that fairytale life with the house, family and picket fence.

"What are your near future plans for my daughter?" daddy questioned.

"My near future plan is to create a beautiful, loving home for our baby and any future children that we'll have."

She Was My Best Friend

"Baby? Tamika are you pregnant?" the way my mother whipped her neck and looked at me was like something from the Exorcist. I cowered beside Christian and pinched him for speed balling.

He just blurted out our secret like it wasn't shit! Didn't he know I was trying to ease into the conversation about being pregnant? This wasn't the build-up to that moment. When I downcast my eyes and got quiet, the answer became loud and clear. Although I've been taking care of myself for a while now, I will always be my parents' baby girl. Disappointment covered their faces and even still, they supported my decision.

"There's nothing we can do because it's already done," walking around the island dad held his hand out. "Welcome to the family son."

Christian stood up as a man and shook my father's hand simultaneously embracing him in a manly hug. The gesture spoke volumes and sealed the deal between two men forming an understanding.

Le'vonne

"Mommy… Dad… Grandmother, I know you guys had high hopes for me and although I'm pregnant that does not negate anything else that I have planned or will do for the matter."

"We know baby girl," Mama walked over and embraced me. "Your father and I raised you right. You have done nothing more than make us proud and we know that you will continue to do so. You have a village and so will our grandchild."

The words my mother spoke warmed my heart. Christian gave a gentle squeeze to my hand and professed his love for me. There was something sexy about a man that had no issue with telling the world how much he loves you.

"I knew you were with child when you walked your shiny face up in here," grandma cackled. "Baby, I hope you have plans to marry her. She will not stay barefoot and pregnant because your loins are sweltering."

Grandma could be a fool when she wanted to, and her antics caused us all to fall out in a fit of laughter. From here on out it was all gas and no breaks. In the short amount of time that it's been since Christian came into my life, I can say for certain that God was showing me that life was too short for regrets and at this point I can honestly say I regret nothing.

Chapter 19:

Brandi

"Mary Ann you better back the fuck up!" with the look of a mother that meant business I dared Mary Ann to charge me if she wanted to. She'd been threatening to hit me for the last hour and I've pretty much had enough.

Today would be the day that I would lose my job because I'm going to flip her ass if she thought she would hit me and get away with it. Disability or not, she know what the fuck she doing. Since the start of my shift she has been cutting the fuck up. Didn't help that I was working by myself because the other staff that now works second shift with me got pulled to another site, and today was Mika's off day.

"I'm telling Mika that you cursed at me!" Mary Ann spat.

She Was My Best Friend

"I don't give a fuck what you tell Mika. You better gone the fuck on." Daring her to take another step, Mary Ann defiantly stared me down before finally retreating to another part of the house. Eleven o'clock couldn't come quick enough. I was ready to go home, wash my ass and go to bed.

Over working all together, I slumped down on the couch and used the remote to turn on the TV. Flipping through the guide channel I decided to watch Botched as the time on my shift wound down. Tonight's episode was about a woman who kept going under the knife to please her man that still left her for someone else. By then she was addicted to being perfect and went overboard with the surgeries. Now she was suffering from botched ass injections and breast implant illness. Shit sounded like my life with Nard minus my surgery being botched.

With thirst getting the better of me, I got up to get a bottle of water from the fridge only to find Mary Ann's funky ass in the kitchen sneaking cupcakes from the pantry. Cursing her the fuck out, I snatched the Hostess box from her clutches and pointed in the direction of her bedroom. She began to yell something about her rights. I politely told her she didn't have any while I was there and proceeded to place the snack back in its rightful place.

After retrieving some h2o I went back into the living room and flopped down onto the couch. Reaching into my purse I pulled out my cell and noticed that I had a missed call from Blaze. We talked here and there since the night we were together, and I'd be lying if I said that I wasn't feeling him. Crazy thing is, it had nothing to do with the fact he gave me a stack. There was just something about him that had my interest piqued. Wanting to hear his voice, I dialed his number and awaited an answer.

"For a minute I thought you was dodging a nigga. What's good B?" Blaze's raspy voice boomed through the phone over the base filled music in his background.

She Was My Best Friend

"Never that. How you been?" Going through the schematics of checking his wellbeing before getting into the meat and potatoes of the conversation. Biting the bullet, I questioned when I'd be able to see him again.

"I plan on coming back up there soon, but say, what's to ole boy that was leaving the house that morning?" Blaze questioned switching the conversation to Stylz.

"That's just my home girl lame ass nigga. He ain't on shit. What's important is how soon is soon in regard to you coming up this way?"

"Tomorrow if you really fucking with me," Blaze's words hung in the air, but they didn't have to stay there long. I admitted that I was fucking with him and would keep my schedule clear just for him.

Ending the call feeling better than I'd felt all day I got back into my program and continued to wait for quitting time.

*

"So, you really fucking with a bitch I see," closing the passenger door I took in Blaze. He was looking and smelling so damn good.

"You looking good beautiful. What you trying to do tonight?"

With a raised eyebrow I shot my shot, "I'm trying to enjoy you in every way I can. What's up?"

"Say less… we can head upstairs and get it cracking," Blaze suggested killing the engine to the car he drove. Tonight he was in an Audi, not the Tesla I remembered.

"Nah, you know I stay with my home girl and she been tripping hard body lately. We can get a room or something."

"I've been meaning to ask you why you didn't have your own place?"

Feeling no ways about speaking my truth, I opened up and told Blaze how I wound up here with Mika. Now that she was acting funny style I was trying to place myself in a position to be in my own and not have to worry about no one else putting me out on my ass. Blaze went on to question what exactly I was doing to put myself in that position and the only option I had was working and told him just that. These days niggas wasn't taking care of bitches like that, or at least that was the problem I've been running into.

"Damn Shorty. From the outside looking in a mafucka wouldn't know you was going through all that. What if I told you, I had a way to get you some quick and easy money with no risk involved?"

My ears perked up at the sounds of what Blaze was kicking. He instructed me to find a hotel room that was out of the way near restaurants and I did just that. On our ride out to Oak Brook he pretty much told me that he was in the business of making money by any means necessary. Sometimes that meant robbing from niggas that was getting it. Honestly I didn't give a fuck how he got his money as long as he was willing to share it with a bitch like me.

After checking into The Hyatt Place, we went to Yorktown Mall to do a little shopping then to McCormick and Schmick's for an early dinner. Blaze had a lot of questions pertaining to Stylz which led me to ask if he was his next mark.

"Look B, nobody is exempt from getting the mask and gloves treatment you feel me? What kind of money that nigga looking at? It's obvious as fuck that he got some money."

Not giving a fuck about setting Christian up, I had to know if that was the reason that Blaze continued to keep in contact with me. I was not about to play myself for a second time on the strength of a nigga.

"Is he the reason why you kept in contact with me?"

"Hell naw! I kept in contact because you fine as hell with some good pussy, plus I could tell that you was a down ass bitch."

Content with his answer I told him what I knew which wasn't much considering he was a topic that me and Mika didn't discuss. He was the reason that our friendship was on thin ice, so I didn't have any issue with the nigga getting robbed. Hell, he robbed me of my only friend so fuck him.

Chapter 20:

Mika

Although my family wasn't excited about me getting pregnant out of wedlock, I was thankful that they were accepting of my relationship with Christian. To know that they were supportive of my decision to carry this child and move in with my baby daddy warmed my heart. There was no doubt that Lovey was going to be overly excited when we tell her. This would be her first grandchild and I was certain that she would spoil the baby with love and gifts.

"I have to stop by my apartment to get some more clothes. You going with me or you just want me to meet you at your moms?"

"You can meet me back here, so we don't have to be in separate cars. I have a run I need to make really quick with my uncle. I'll be back home around two-ish. Sound good to you?"

"Yep. I can work with that." Kissing Christian seductively, I rolled out of bed and sauntered to the bathroom.

By the time I turned on the shower and stepped in, Christian was behind me following suit. Backing me up against the wall, he continued the kiss I initiated in the bedroom. Wrapping my arms around his neck, he hoisted me up and slid me onto his erect pole. Slowly I wound my middle while he gripped my ass and guided me to bounce up and down switching up the tempo.

"You love me bae?"

"Yes!" I answered loving the way he tickled my middle. It wasn't going to be long before my love rained down.

"Can I have you forever?" Christian held me taut as he slid in and out slowly. Again my answer was yes.

"Will you allow me to provide and protect you and our kids by any means necessary?"

Nodding my head yes I was on the brink of a beautiful explosion. When he asked me to marry him I screamed out yes, more in regard to the nut I was busting and not to his question. Covering my mouth with his, I digested what I'd just agreed to as our tongues intertwined. Horror set in as the realization that he asked me to marry him and I said yes. Lord help me. Everything was moving too fast but there was no way I could retract my answer.

Christian cried real tears as he stood me up and gazed into my eyes. Turning my head away because I felt that he would know I wasn't so sure otherwise; I grabbed my loofah and poured my favorite body wash onto it. Taking the loofah from my hand, Christian asked if I was sure. Unable to break his heart I nodded yes.

"Tamika stop lying to me. Is this something that you want? Honestly?"

She Was My Best Friend

"I do everything is just moving so fast," I admitted.

"It doesn't have to happen tomorrow. I just want to assure you that you have my heart and I'm yours until the day after forever. I ain't going nowhere. Even if you wake up tomorrow and decide you don't want me I'll still take care of you and my child."

"Baby, please understand that I do want to marry you. I love you with all of my heart and soul. I'm just scared because everything has been moving so quickly between us. One thing about it, I'm learning to trust the process and in doing so I accept your proposal."

For a moment Christian studied me, "Don't tell me that just to make me feel better."

"I mean it. Christian I will marry you and I want a big ass ring."

The smile that graced my face was all the confirmation he needed. We would have fucked again if he didn't need to meet his uncle. Agreeing to take me ring shopping soon we washed away our interlude with a promise that we would meet up later today.

*

"I wasn't expecting to see you here," Brandi leaned on the doorjamb to my bedroom with her arms crossed.

To say the lines of communication have been blurred between us is an understatement. Here I am happier than I've ever been, and I haven't been able to share any of it with my best friend and that shit was bothering me.

"We need to talk," I admitted placing the last article of clothing into my bag. Pretty soon, I'll be packing up my entire apartment and before that came to fruition we were going to need to iron out whatever our issue was.

"Now you want to talk," Brandi's words dripped with sarcasm. "When I tried to talk to your ass you wanted to be all professional and not do it because we were at work. I guess this is a safe space, huh?"

"Brandi will you turn your gangster the fuck down!" Beginning to become frustrated I almost said fuck it but there are some things I needed to get off my chest. "Look, either we about to fix what's wrong or we just not going to fuck with each other. I love you like you're my sister, but I don't have time for no bullshit B."

"Pull your granny panties out your ass Mika damn! Your ass ain't fun no more. You always so serious, please chill out ma'am."

Taking a deep breath I waited for Brandi to take a seat at the foot of my bed before I spoke. "Bitch I'm pregnant!"

I don't know if the look on her face was one of disbelief or disdain. Either way I didn't like it. Seconds seemed like hours as I awaited a response from her.

"Why you sitting here bullshitting?"

"On my mama. I'm six weeks and we've decided to get married."

Brandi fell out into a fit of laughter as if something was funny. Taken aback by her actions I had to ask what I had said that had her so tickled.

"The more I teach you the dumber you get. You really think this nigga going to marry you? Bitch please. He done knocked you up and about to use your ass as his little toy until he tired of playing with you. Should've made that nigga strap up and how y'all getting married and you don't even have a ring on your finger. Let me guess… it's on layaway?"

"Hoe if I didn't know any better I'd believe that you don't even fuck with me like that! No matter what stupid ass shit you did or allowed a nigga to do to you never have I come out of my mouth and talked down to you or even laughed in your face. Guess what mafuckas saying is true."

She Was My Best Friend

"What the fuck is people saying about me?" Brandi stopped laughing to question what the rumor mill had swirling about her.

"It don't even matter. Just know when a person show me the real them, I believe it. My lease about to be over soon and I'm moving so you need to figure out your life."

My feelings were so hurt but I refused to show it. Junie, my mama, my grandma and even Christian told me about the bitch Brandi, but I didn't want to believe it. I let the years we had together and my loyalty blind me from the bitch she truly was. She ain't' never fuck with me the same way I fucked with her. Like the old adage goes, when you know better you do better. I can't do shit but take this as a lesson learned and move on with my life.

"Wow… you just like everybody else. Fuck you Tamika. I'll be out of your shit tonight and I quit!" Brandi stormed out of the room and moments later I heard the front door slam.

Le'vonne

By the time we made it to Christian's mother's house I was all the way in my feelings. On the entire ride over, he kept asking me what was wrong and of course I told him nothing. I didn't have the mental capacity to deal with another I told you so in regard to Brandi, so I held that shit to my chest. Somehow I was able to push that episode with Brandi to the back of my mind and go on with my afternoon. Just like we thought, Lovey was over the moon with excitement to learn that she was about to be a grandmother and truly gaining a daughter. She fed me so much and I knew this was going to become my norm for the whole pregnancy. She was going to have me big as a damn house.

Realizing that I left my damn phone at the house, I told Christian that I'd have to run back home to get it. Although it could have waited until we were on our way home, I was using my phone as an excuse to go out and clear my mind. Even with the amount of love that was enveloping me here, the breakup of my friendship with Brandi hurt like hell.

She Was My Best Friend

"We can just head out and get your phone then go home," Christian suggested, "I'm tired anyway plus I want to enjoy the rest of the night loving on you."

Knowing he wasn't going to let up I agreed. Saying our goodbye's to Christian's family Lovey sent us home with more food than we needed but we allowed her to be great. On the ride back to my apartment I wound up telling him what occurred with me, and Brandi earlier today. In normal fashion, he supported my decision to not fuck with her anymore rather than hit me with an *I told you so.* For that I was grateful. Having gotten my feelings off my chest, I felt a little bit better, but I knew that it would take some time to get over a twenty-four-year friendship.

Christian chose to sit in his car while I ran up to get my phone. As much as my phone stay glued to my hand, that whole little spat had me absent minded. When I got upstairs Brandi was in the spare bedroom packing up her things. *Good riddance,* I thought rolling my eyes as I kept stepping towards my room. I hadn't a clue where she was going, and I really didn't give a damn. Grabbing the reason for my return I left just as quietly as I had come in, not bothering to say a damn thing to Brandi.

For some reason or another I felt the urge to hurry down the stairs in an attempt to get far away from the negative energy permeating in the air. Never in my wildest dreams did I think I'd walk out of my apartment building and find Christian with a gun in his face just as the gunman let off two shots. Screaming in horror the gunman turned in my direction and let off another round piercing my chest. As I fell to the ground, I could feel my life slipping away as everything went black.

Chapter 21:

Brandi

Since my friendship was over with Mika it only made sense for me to get up out of her house. There was no need to sit around and wait on her to kick me out on my ass, this time I was leaving with grace and dignity. Thank God for Blaze, although I didn't know him from shit I felt like we could really build. When he offered for me to come out to the D I didn't have shit to lose as I agreed. His lifestyle wasn't stellar, but I done dealt with killers, drug dealers and robbers before. I needed a new lease on life, and it seemed like he was going to be the one to give me just that even if I had to help him set niggas up.

Packing up my shit, Tamika came in to get something I supposed because the bitch left just as quickly as she came. By tomorrow morning she wouldn't have to worry about me because I'll be on my way to Detroit with Blaze being the Bonnie to his Clyde.

Pop…pop…pop the sound of gunshots wasn't an uncommon thing when you lived in the hood but something about the time they occurred didn't sit well with me. The noise was too close for comfort and although my bedroom wasn't facing the front of the building that was the direction the sound came from. Quickly I walked towards the living room to take a look outside and my fucking heart fell out my chest. Mika lie on her back in front of the building in a pool of blood while Stylz's body hung haphazardly out of his car lifeless.

Letting out a blood-curdling scream I rushed out of the apartment and ran down the stairs as fast as I could. By the time I reached the main level my legs felt as if I was walking through quick sand. The only person that gave a fuck about me lay on the dirty concrete teetering between life and death. All the shit

She Was My Best Friend

I'd said and done to Mika began to plague me. I threw away a lifelong friendship because I was jealous and now she was lying on the ground fighting for her life. Falling to my knees I placed my hands over the bullet hole in Mika's chest in an attempt to stop the blood from flowing.

"Hold on Mika… please hold on," I cried as she looked up at me. Terror was written on her face as I begged her to hold on. Sirens can be heard in the distance as neighbors began to come out of their homes offering whatever help they could.

"NOOOOOOOOO   MIKA NOOOOOOOOOOOO," tears poured from my eyes as she took her last breath and urinated.

"She gone," someone whispered in an attempt to pull me off of her as I began to give her mouth-to-mouth and chest compressions. She couldn't be gone. She was only twenty-four years old. She had much more life to live. She had a baby on the way…

Le'vonne

The cops began to tape off the scene just as the ambulance arrived. Although it was apparent that both Mika and Stylz were dead the paramedics had to call it. Feeling like absolute shit I regretted every foul thing that occurred over the years. I was never good enough to be her friend, yet she loved me unconditionally no matter what shit came with me. Somehow I was able to dial up Ms. Janet to give her the horrible news about her one and only child. The way she screamed through the phone caused my guilt to eat me up all the more.

"Excuse me miss but I have a few questions for you," a female detective approached me as I sat on the curb balling my eyes out. "Do you know the victims?"

I let the detective know that I did and gave her the information that she required minus who had done it. Although I wanted to believe that this was a random accident, my common sense wouldn't allow it. Mika never bothered anybody and from what I know Stylz only flipped properties, he wasn't a well-known nigga in these streets doing normal hood nigga shit like drug dealing. He got his money legitimately but that didn't matter to a stickup kid. Giving me a business card, the detective allowed me a moment and let me know that they may very well need to speak with me at a later time at the precinct. In the meantime, if I remember anything to give her a call.

My heart broke all over again when Mika's family arrived at the scene. Her mother ran over to where Mika lay lifeless covered in a white sheet. The cops tried to keep her back, but their attempts were met with a mother's will to see her child. The way Mrs. Lewis collapsed to the ground hurt my soul. This shit was my fault. Knowing that slowly killed me.

"We got a lead on the shooter," a young white detective approached the one I'd just been talking to and called himself whispering to her. "The witnesses said it was an African American male in a black Audi truck."

Le'vonne

Hearing that description confirmed that it was Blaze. He should have been back at the hotel, not staking out the apartment. I left him under the premise that I was coming to get my things so that we could head to Detroit first thing in the morning. Did he think I wouldn't give him the drop? Furthermore, why would he shoot Mika? She didn't deserve what happened to her.

Pulling out my cell I dialed Blaze's number only to be met with the voicemail greeting. Again and again I dialed his number and got the same outcome. Dipping away from the scene I raced upstairs to get my car keys. Securing the house I slipped back out of the building and down the street to my car. Still feeling fucked up because I couldn't even bring myself to be there for Mika's people. With shaky hands I started up my car. Pulling out of the park, I reversed to the corner and hit the side street. Racing towards the expressway my phone began to ring. Hoping it was Blaze, I looked at the screen then tossed it into the passenger seat when I saw Junie's name. There was no time to chat, nor offer any information. Certainly by now she was aware of Mika's demise.

In under an hour I was walking into the lobby of Hyatt Place. There was no need for me to go up to the desk I already had a key card to the room. Taking the elevator up to the eighth floor I got off and proceeded to room eight zero eight. Placing the key card into the door the light turned from red to green allowing access. Walking into the room it was apparent that Blaze was gone. The bed was still disheveled from our earlier tryst and the bag he had off in the corner was now gone. Defeated I sat at the foot of the bed and called his phone for the millionth time still garnering the same results. With my head in my hands I cried like I'd never cried before. My best friend was dead, and my savior left me high and dry.

*

"I'm coming live to you from Cook County Jail where Thomas Knight, the suspect who allegedly shot and killed twenty-seven-year-old Christian Myles and twenty-four-year-old Tamika Jones just one week ago in a robbery gone wrong has been arraigned. Mr. Knight who is a known criminal from Detroit allegedly came here to Chicago to meet with get this, a friend of Ms. Jones and together the two of them conspired to rob Mr. Myles. The identity of the friend is unknown at this time, but we'll keep you posted as details become clear to us. Back to you Don."

In shock I sat listening to the news anchor. Blaze's bitch ass got caught and couldn't take the heat by his damn self. It was a no brainer that I needed to get the fuck out of dodge before the cops came knocking at my mother's door. With no time to pack up anything I grabbed a couple of jogging suits and prepared to leave. There was no way in hell I was going to jail. Descending the stairs with a book bag over my shoulder, my mother was standing at the door with two men in suits. It didn't take a rocket scientist to know that they were here for me.

With nowhere to go I succumbed to my fate. Dropping the bag on the stairs I walked over to my crying mother and told her I loved her and that I was sorry for disappointing her. The detectives read me my Miranda rights as they cuffed and escorted me to a waiting Impala. Hot tears stung my face knowing that my life was completely over for no reason other than that green-eyed monster envy. I was used to being the '*It girl*' now I was the girl that got her friend killed by default, all because she had a nigga that was giving her what I once had. Jealousy was a bitch.

The End

Check out the rest of the Ex-Best Friend Series on Amazon

BRAND BULLIES PUBLISHING PRESENTS
BackStabbers
SHE WAS MY BEST FRIEND
ROBIN

BRAND BULLIES PUBLISHING PRESENTS
Betrayed
SHE WAS MY BEST FRIEND
DANI K

BRAND BULLIES PUBLISHING PRESENTS
Two-Faced
SHE WAS MY BEST FRIEND
KATRINA LEE

www.ingramcontent.com/pod-product-compliance
Lightning Source LLC
Chambersburg PA
CBHW061250120726
48001CB00001B/242